P. A. STAES

a novel

The BRUGES TAPESTRY

TapissierMedia

Los Angeles · New York · Brussels

The Bruges Tapestry is a work of historical fiction. While certain historical persons and events are mentioned, their activities are entirely fictional. All names, characters, places, and incidents are a product of the author's work. Any resemblance to current events, persons, or locales is entirely coincidental.

For the sake of pacing, the time period for weaving a tapestry has been compressed in this novel.

Book Design: Eddie Vincent, ENC Graphic Services
Cover design: Kathi Dunn, www.dunn-design.com
Author photograph by Linda Joseph, SilverMoon Photography

Grateful acknowledgement is made to the following for permission to print previously published material:
Vittoria Colonna, Marchesa di Pescara (1490/92-1547). Amaro Lagrimar. The Poems of Vittoria Colonna, Newly Translated and Arranged by Ellen Moody. Translations and notes copyright © Ellen Moody 1997, 1998, 1999, 2000, 2001, 2002, 2003, 2004. http://www.jimandellen.org/vcpoetry/vctitle.htm

Dedication

To Rick, for your love and hard work,
and to Lois Jean Wallner (1939-2009) -
I miss you every day.

Acknowledgements

Many thanks to Stella Togo, book coach extraordinaire, for shepherding me through the publishing process. Her unflagging enthusiasm is an inspiration. Thanks also to Kathi Dunn for the thrilling book cover design. Kudos to William Tucker for editing out my more egregious errors (any remaining are entirely my responsibility). To Linda Joseph, of SilverMoon Photography, I'm grateful for her spirit of joy during our sessions.

I would like to recognize Louise Martin and her co-weavers at Stirling Castle, Stirling, Scotland for tapestry information and for their warm welcome while I sat observed them weaving in the castle's Nether Bailey.

Thank you also to the following for invaluable assistance: Detective Donald Hrycyk of the Los Angeles Police Department's art theft detail for entertaining questions about art theft; Drea Lead (Elizabethan costume expert) and Gary Pattillo (University of North Carolina at Chapel Hill) for costuming of the 16th century; Sharon Upp for spiritual guidance; Carol Gergen, who inspired the antics of Nora Fitzsimmons; Dieter Viaene, of Mechelen, for information on Charles V; Geraldine F. Clarke for Latin Translations; and reference librarian, Gayle Meldau, at the City of Mission Viejo Library for everything, especially for Hugh Rawson's great book, Wicked Words.

My gratitude is extended to Ellen Moody, translator of the poetry of Vittoria Colona, for permission to use translated material.

And to Kris Neri, writer and teacher, thank you for the tools.

Table of Contents

The Juniper Tree

See that lovely juniper, pressed so hard,
angry winds swirl round her, but she'll not let
her leaves fall or scatter; clenched, branches held
high, she gathers strength; her refuge within.

This, my friend, is a picture of my soul
standing firm against all; if life's ravaged,
weakened me, my fear's contained, and I win
by enduring a pain which makes it hurt

to breathe. Mine was a noble dream, sheltered
in his splendor and love, my pride would be
restored; I would encounter life's bitter

battles. Nature taught this tree to resist:
in me you see what reason can perform
how from the worst evil good can grow.

Vittoria Colonna, Marchesa di Pescara (1490/92-1547).

1520 Bruges, Beligium

I was sixteen years old when Marie died giving birth to Father Bernardo's child. I had not known the day I opened the door to him, when he came in along with the stench of the canals, that he would betray my sister's trust. He came to 'hear her confession' and made a sinner of her instead.

CHAPTER ONE

Claire, the Present

I can't get it out of my mind. I've tried to forget, forget losing the best friend I ever had. It was such an ordinary day, an ordinary plan: lunch and then a party. Or so it seemed ordinary at the time.

But here's the rub: Nora, my friend, is not ordinary. I'm the ordinary one, or as a friend once reminded me, a white-bread kind of person. And who, I ask you, wants to be a white-bread kind of person? Or befriend one?

Nora was my alter ego. All hyperbole, display, sparkle. I was her straight man. I'm not now. I'm not anything to her now. No, that's not true. Nora hates me, little ole white-bread-me. And as I said, it seemed like such an ordinary day, that day starting with lunch.

"I thought you weren't going to sleep with Italian men anymore." I waited for Nora's response. I was playing with my iced tea, spinning the cubes around with the straw, catching mint in the tip, and then blowing it out with an embarrassing noise.

"When did I say that?" Nora asked. She crossed her long, oiled legs and leaned into the caned back of the bamboo chair.

Nora was checking out the action at our favorite lunch spot: an upscale Newport Beach restaurant with a Gauguinesque décor. Bamboo, palm trees and bird of paradise surrounded the tables. Chairs were clad in a Hawaiian print style of the 1940s.

I loved the décor's camp, Polynesian theme. Stalks of fake wooden bananas sat atop the bar where row after row of polished glasses hung upside down from an overhead bamboo rack, ready for the bartender's touch. Above the rack were various Polynesian accoutréments: sculptures of reclining semi-nude island women, fake pineapples, ceramic fish. Newport Beach businessmen lined the bar; their jackets hung limply like wounded soldiers over the backs of bar chairs.

"Hmm—Let me see. When was that?" I pretended to make a mental journey into the not-so-long-ago conversation. "I know. It was the night we rented that Italian movie."

For years we had discussed sex, men, art, politics and popular culture. Today I was attempting to flush out information about Nora's latest arm candy. I am, after all, a detective—or had I failed to mention that?

While I waited, I reviewed Nora's ensemble for the day—the cheetah look. Nora Fitzsimmons, you see, is an incandescent mix of the sublime and the ridiculous—well-suited to a career as an interior designer. The cheetah look complemented Nora's brown eyes and blond hair. There was a brownish-yellow theme. She had, no doubt, planned it.

"Oh, that movie," Nora hollered. She waved the fork dismissively, and a tiny hunk of salmon took flight. She appeared to be making a design out of the food on her plate, artfully arranging it on the pineapple motif. With the palm trees framing her and the cheetah attire, I thought of a Rousseau painting.

When my attention turned back to her, Nora was explaining herself. There was a bit of mumbling with food in her mouth, but I caught the end of the sentence, "…I've changed my mind."

"Oh?" I said it as if this were news. It wasn't, so I continued to gaze about the room. It was a warm day, and the ceiling fans circled like turkey vultures.

"It just so happens that an Italian man owns the place I'm working on now."

"Yes." I waited again. Describing her love life brought out the best in Nora. It was like having lunch with Dorothy Parker. I wanted details. I stopped looking at the ceiling fans.

"His name is Paolo Campezzi. He looks like Viggo Mortensen and…," Nora lifted scrupulously waxed eyebrows for emphasis while leaning forward to whisper the last bit.

I interrupted. "Viggo who? Oh, the actor-poet with the cleft chin."

I couldn't conjure the entire face, but the cleft chin was unforgettable. Saying that Paolo looked like Viggo was a short-cut for 'very hot' and 'a bit of a mumbler.'

"You would like Paolo, Claire. He's kind, warm, funny and compassionate. Isn't it just an amazing coincidence that he's sexy, rich, gorgeous, Italian and pedigreed?" She seemed extremely pleased with the string of adjectives she'd just compiled, like a linguistic necklace.

"Uh huh," I had heard this refrain before. The ceiling fans became more interesting again.

"What are you doing tonight?" she asked as the waiter poured more iced tea, which gave me some time to make up a cheap excuse. I had to think quickly. *God! No parties. Please.*

Nora glanced at the waiter's ass but he looked a bit young, even for her. The waiters here were indeed young and, though the theme of the restaurant was Polynesian, someone had decided they should wear Hemingway garb. This gave the place an odd ambience of a safari in Hawaii. I had a mental picture of rhinos running down Waikiki Beach.

"Why?" The word came out with more irritation than I intended. *Shit. It was the wrong answer.* I knew I should have said I was taking Leila to the vet, or washing my hair, or watching a PBS special on whales. Hell's bells.

Nora wasn't looking at me. She was scrutinizing the men at the bar while pretending to attend to her nails. "Don't sound so suspicious. I just wanted to remind you about the party. Paolo wants to show off his house. I think he wants to show me off too. Please come."

Why, oh why, did Nora need me to go? Moral support? Nora loved these Newport Beach parties, though at heart she felt a bit inferior to the wealthy women who spent their spare time as docents at various Newport museums, and lacked anything more challenging in their day than finding nail polish to match their sports cars. I had told her before I couldn't stand that level of self-absorption. I truly hated the parties. My beige-ness seemed glaring at those times.

"Leila needs to be de-wormed," I lied as I waded through my purse, feigning a pen hunt. I knew it was lame. Even Nora could sniff out lame. My leg was shaking up and down where I had placed it across my knee. I could probably get to the restroom before she could reply.

"Liar! Come on! It's my best job yet. You need to see it."

"I've seen your work, Nora. I see your work all the time. You did my apartment, remember?"

Like Nora would forget. We had been at it for months. Nora had made my above-the-garage apartment in Corona del Mar funky, warm and anything but beige.

Nora faked a French accent. "Yes, but in zis case we're talking thousand-count sheets, not a 50-50 blend from Tarzhay."

Okay, so I didn't have any inherent taste of my own. Sometimes I worried I didn't have any inherent personality either—just a reflection of the world around me or the people I envied. That seemed too pathetic so I put it out of my mind. It wasn't like Nora could pick up a personality for me while shopping for towels.

While furnishing my apartment, Nora brought art, lamps, and pillows to me in the evening—usually items rejected by a wealthy client. My favorite piece was a work of art mounted on the pale mustard-colored living room wall. Within a gold frame two women peered out. The work looked medieval until you came up close. The head and shoulders of the two women were robed in deep red wool and there were ruffled wimples hiding their hair, surrounding pale, bird-like faces.

Those figures hinted at a sad story, perhaps a tragic one.

This appealed to me. I like tragedy, interesting tragedy. I'm not saying I like multiple vehicle accidents with fatalities, more like tragic tales of the human condition.

I had some odd connection to medieval times which I couldn't explain. I felt close to those 'birdish' women and their hidden tragedy.

Pulling myself back to the current discussion of Paolo's abode I ventured, "Well I wouldn't want to miss those sheets. How often does one get to stare at sheets they'll never sleep on?" I slumped a bit in the chair just to let her know I would make her pay.

"Oh! Ending a sentence with a preposition! What's happening to you? I thought you were a grammarian in your former life. Didn't Sister Mary Almond Roca teach you grammar?"

I snorted inadvertently, and a bit of mint from the iced tea seemed to be stuck in my nose. My interminable parochial education was fair game always. "A grammarian? No, that was linguistics. I studied linguistics, not grammar, in college. And I didn't have a Sister Mary Almond Roca for grammar. I think it was Sister Orange Julius."

Nora hooted while rocking back and forth. "Oh God, Our Lady of Perpetual Ingratitude will dry up your womb for that remark." Honestly, does God strike down ex-Catholics for laughing at things like this? I couldn't help myself. Snot, tears, iced tea and mint seemed to accumulate under my nose. My friends tell me I'm a class act.

Wiping my nose and regaining some self-control, I said, "That womb hasn't been busy lately anyway." Nora wiped her eyes. "You're my best audience. No one else laughs at every word I utter."

"Listen," she moved her chair up closer. There was a laissez-faire hand wave to dismiss my building angst. "I don't care about the sheets, and neither do you. It's the tapestry I want you to see. I told you about the tapestry. It's a sixteenth-century Flemish or Dutch work or something like that. It's one of those cold, flat countries in the middle of Europe, where everyone has a ruddy complexion. You're Flemish aren't you?"

"Yes. What's that got to do with it?" Why should I go to a party to see a tapestry? That was like saying I should polka to work if my grandparents were Polish.

"Nothing—it's just that Paolo is so proud of the place and of that tapestry in particular. I want you to see my work. The art he has is spectacular, and I've hung it magnificently." She nodded in agreement with herself.

"Humility being your strong suit...."

"Oh, you're an art freak, you'll love it." Nora moved the empty plate aside, picking up the dessert menu. We had a plan to save calories for dessert. The strategy evaporated during appetizers.

"I'll tell you, it's a good thing you're an art cop and not a regular cop," Nora continued. She'd said 'cop' so loudly I could see heads turn. Men at the bar looked straight in my direction. *Oh hell.* "Then we'd have dinner over terms like 'self-defenestration.' That kind of thing would interfere with my appetite."

"You're right," I nodded at the dessert menu, "there aren't many art thieves throwing themselves out windows these days, and God forbid that I should interfere with your appetite." Nora maintained a voluptuous, albeit middle-aged body, probably via thousands of sex partners. Well, maybe I exaggerate. It just felt like that compared with my love life.

I sighed and rolled my eyes. I practiced not looking pleased. I may have placed my arms akimbo just to look grumpy. "Ok, let me get this straight. I go to the party in Newport Beach to look at a tapestry. That should take about 15 minutes. Can I go home then?" I was reluctant to be sucked into a vortex of vapid women discussing their plastic surgeons' asses.

Nora pinched my cheeks.

"Remember when your mother pinched your cheeks to give you color? Come on, get excited. Claire, you might actually meet someone like Paolo. He has friends all over Newport."

Yeah, I could just imagine Paolo's friends. I had dated one or two of Nora's suggestions but found them to be like crème brûlée: smooth, but a dangerous habit to develop.

Then I heard Nora's gentle voice and felt her hand on my arm. The playful tone was gone, her voice warm, reassuring. "This thing you have for your boss is not going anywhere, Claire. Come on, it's been a year since Simon went back to his wife. He wasn't and isn't for you. You deserve someone who cherishes you."

There it was—the plain truth. The one I didn't want to hear. I picked at the crumbs on the tablecloth. I moved them into a tidy pile. I stacked the pile into three little piles. I pressed my lips together in order to stop that hot feeling you get when tears start in your eyes and drop into your smarting nose.

I noticed the sad orchid in the center of the table, oddly alone in its arrangement and clearly past its prime. I contemplated ripping its pathetic blossoms to shreds.

Nora forged ahead. "Claire, Simon isn't the love of your life. He's the love of your fantasy life. There's a difference."

That hurt. I made a show of rubbing my nose, and smacked at the table crumbs—my gesture of finality and resolve.

"OK, why not. I'll go. Did you say seven? Can I come straight from work?"

"No you can't come straight from work! Wear something very small and black." Oy, there was the look of determination on Nora's face. She didn't like my linen work suits.

"I'm not sure about the small, but I'll be there in black at seven." There must be something appropriate in the closet, but had it been manufactured in the last decade, I wondered. I looked around the restaurant, but the men at the bar had long since turned back to their lunch-time drinks after hearing I was a cop and seeing that I didn't look butch enough to be one. I was safe from having to demonstrate my prowess.

Nora smiled triumphantly and paid the bill. Her every move was monitored by two men at an adjacent table. I couldn't tell if it was Nora's cheetah micro-miniskirt or the matching faux-bone bracelets, clanging a cannibalistic tune, that held their attention. I had often heard Nora say that all jewelry should be large enough to make noise, so no exit goes unnoticed. And it did not.

Chapter Two

Beatrice in 1520

I write this for Marie, and I hide it for myself. Death awaits me if this is found. Though I am but sixteen, I think of death now every day.

I begin quickly in order to end quickly. If these writings are found, please, I beg you, set right the wrongs herein.

My sister and I worked in the shop of our Father, Cornelius van Hecke, one of the finest tapestry weavers in Bruges. We worked among twelve weaving apprentices. I write we worked there. The tapisserie no longer exists. I am the only one left. They are all gone. My Father is gone. All twelve apprentices—dead. Gone.

In better times Marie and I brought lunch to Father daily and sat with him as he spoke with the Italian gentlemen who brought in the cartoons: the drawings to place behind the tapestries so the design can be woven. Our Father was an excellent businessman with a growing reputation for skill and honesty.

When we were very young, Marie and I sat under

the weavers' benches watching them from below the loom, whispering and laughing at our own childish ideas about them. Sometimes we hid their scissors and they complained loudly to Father about it. Well, Basil Cœke complained. Jan van Leyden just laughed. Basil smelled bad, and he had rotting teeth and a pitted nose. Jan had lovely calves and was smitten with Marie. He would wink at her under the bench and sometimes pass small gifts or treats to her. I kicked her until she gave me half her treasure: a bun or a piece of fruit.

Adolph, Dominicus and Mauritius worked with us as well but were older, at least by ten years, and quieter. They left us to our play. The others were older still with brown, furrowed skin and large veins in the back of their hands. They appeared not to hear as well as the younger men. Gustaf, Alfons, Achiel, Willem, Francois, Johannes—all were hunched in the back but were known masters of their craft.

Father oversaw every aspect of the work at the tapisserie. He watched as the loom was set up and as the woolen warp threads were rolled onto the beam away from the weaver.

When we were young, Father taught us about his craft. He said, "The warp threads will be as long as the finished tapestry. The longest tapestry I know of is from Brussels and is one hundred meters long!" Marie and I took turns racing one hundred meters to know the length and to find a winner. We could think of nothing we knew so long, except perhaps ten castle gates end-to-end.

Sometimes Jan raced with us, but he won too frequently so we made him watch instead or carry us over the finish line. Father would admonish us to behave as ladies while Jan reddened and returned to his bench. I thought Marie giggled far too much when Jan picked her up, and I told her so.

Father traveled to see the work of other masters, such as Pieter de Pannemaker who worked on tapestries for Emperor Maximilian in Brussels. Father was also a great admirer of Pieter van Aelst who was creating a work depicting the Acts of the Apostles.

We asked many questions when we were very young. Why did loops run down from each warp thread? What were the wooden slats below? How did the colored threads in baskets on the floor turn into pictures on fabric? Why were the cartoons cut into pieces?

"You girls!" he said, pretending to be annoyed, "You bring too many questions with my waterzooi. I will have to send you home to get any work done." But he always answered the questions with a joyous aspect while we watched him pull at the dark bread and scoop from the pot of chicken, carrots, potatoes and leeks Mother had sent with us.

After a deep sigh of feigned annoyance followed by tickling, he pointed, "The loops run down to heddling bars under foot. There are bars for even and odd threads and the weaver can step on the bars to separate the loops into a shed. The shed is that space you see between the threads when the weaver steps on the heddling bar. Then the colored thread on the shuttles is threaded through the shed." It was an explanation that befuddled me, but I did see the opening in the warp to allow the weft threads to pass through—so that must have been the shed.

He pointed while the workers demonstrated for us. I was allowed to put a shuttle with bright red thread through the shed.

"The cartoons are the paper drawings of what is woven into the tapestry. They are cut into strips so the weaver can place them under the warp. This way the weaver can look through the warp to see the design."

He added that in certain types of weaving the words on the cartoon must be reversed in order to come out properly on the tapestry. If the cartoon artists forgot to make a mirror image, then the weavers' lettering would come out reversed on the tapestry.

We covered our mouths, laughing until our starched linen caps shook. Backward words! That day Marie and I practiced writing backward all day. Marie sent notes to Jan with careful backward script. I saw him give her a nod and half a smile and place the note inside his cloak. She giggled and touched her cap.

Mother made us stop writing to help make dinner. On one of Father's travels to Brussels, he had brought home a most precious gift to mother: a cookbook. Mother was an excellent cook, but books were highly valued. This was no small gift. It described forty ways to cook fish!

Mother, Marie and I looked at it often together, but most of the foodstuffs were too dear for us to afford. *A Notable Little Cookery Book* sat on the kitchen shelf where the three of us could practice recipes fit for kings, when we could afford the ingredients. I was proud that our family owned a book. Only the notable gentlemen of our town, including the more successful artisans and merchants, could afford a book.

Mother, Marie and I practiced tarts and jams on light days in the tapisserie. There were so many things we had never heard of or would never find in the market such as figs, marzipan, peacocks, and ginger. We could only imagine where these items could be obtained and how they would come to the market from a land so far away where the residents there might have fur or horns! The cookbook also gave recipes for one of Father's favorite meals from Brussels: *whelk*, also known as sea snail.

We looked for ways to flavor food we ate during the five months a year when some type of religious fasting was required. Then we ate only bread, vegetables and fish. Many of the recipes concerned the fasting period when no meat or dairy products could be consumed. Marie, Mother and I had plenty of practice with those recipes.

Marie and I loved our city, and we would explore it together when Mother allowed us to do the marketing. It was a city of browns, just like the floors and walls of the tapisserie. The cobblestones were tan and the small bridges over the canals were grayish-brown, though the canals themselves had a green tinge so that the tiny bridges seemed to be reins crisscrossing over a dragon's back. The lazy, sleepy dragon was made up of the green canals, and the bridges bent over the dragon's verdigris back.

If Marie and I were on the canals in the evening studying the night sky, we were most certainly chaperoned by Father. God had hurled the stars above us sometimes in clumps and sometimes individually. They formed a brilliant path above us to reflect on the dark cobblestones below.

Bruges was a town defined by water. The canals were the catch basins for the water from the frequent rains. On occasion the brown walls above the canals were brightened by red geraniums hanging over window boxes. Those geraniums were carefully tended and saved in winter windows year after year so that they could make their summer excursion to the outdoor window boxes.

The Stadhuis, our town hall, was imposingly grey with a great, orangish-brown oak ceiling. Marie and I would race around the spire-topped hall exterior to the market, Grote Markt, and back.

These are joys of old, no longer part of my life. Marie, Mother, Father, and the graceful and smitten Jan are all dead.

When Mother died of ague, with fever and sweating

she did nothing to deserve, Father let Marie and I stay at the tapisserie most days. Eventually we began to work on the weavings. I think Father felt less lonely when we were there. At least he believed we were safe.

Work filled the lost space in all of us. Father would tolerate no talk of grief over Mother, but I added sage to his food to allay his sick emotion. His pain was so intense that any mention of Mother sent him into tears and he spent days without speaking.

Our tapisserie was a home of stone walls, black with soot from the fire. Even during cold weather, shutters and windows were kept open to allow the stifling air to escape. Twelve men, for there were that many in total during rushed times, could create great noise and body heat. Sometimes my sister and I pinched our noses at their musky smell and terrible noises and flatulence of the bowels. Their emanations could be quite foul: a combination of body sweat, wood smoke on their clothing, and other mysterious odors. We could not identify these stenches but surmised they must be unique to grown men.

The tapisserie was our haven for safety and warmth. The guild allowed work only during the daylight hours. Marie and I could creep in at night while the air smelled of wool and sometimes of the woad and urine used to dye wool blue. Still, we could be lulled to peaceful sleep underneath the looms when a fading sun cast pink light on small panes of wavy window glass.

Though only one year older at sixteen, Marie became like a mother to me over time. Yet, she led me to mischief too. She was adept at escaping responsibility for her petty crimes in the tapisserie—most involving tormenting Jan—or better yet, Basil "Meniere Cabbage Face" as Marie called him behind his back.

Marie possessed the countenance of an angel, and Father believed every word she uttered to him. I was easily convinced to do her bidding and pay the consequences.

That year Marie and I grew old enough to be married, but Father was too busy at work to make marriage alliances with other guildsmen. I would not have married, even if he had made such bargains. I felt it was my place to care for Father, as Marie cared for me.

I believed then that Marie would marry one day. She was the beautiful one—clear skin, straight nose and laughing green eyes. She looked like Father, but held herself upright with the pride of Mother's family. Marie's golden brown hair was waist long, squeezing out of the linen cap at the nape of her neck. She had developed the body of a woman. I had not. A woman's body may have been her undoing. I learned this soon enough when two strangers entered the shop—nearly a year before this writing.

CHAPTER THREE

Claire at Work

I left Nora at the restaurant's front door, reiterating my promise to attend the party. She entered her sage-green Jaguar. Jaguar and cheetah—her feline obsessions. I gave a half-assed wave. I really could just spit. A Newport Beach party was not exactly my style.

Exiting the restaurant door, I passed under green canvas awnings announcing the names of the various businesses. There was the dog bone boutique, Bone Appetit, where I bought Leila a bag of mint-flavored bones. Progress along the sidewalk brought Gelato Paradiso into sight. The green awning at GP sported a large white blob on the green background. This must have been intended to be a cone topped with gelato.

I decided to get a cup of gelato before going up the hill to the office. Behind the counter was a cute, college-athlete type wearing an Alabama T-shirt, sporting buzzed hair and the kind of earring that makes progressively larger holes in the earlobe until one can pass a Buick through the lobe.

Twenty-four flavors of the smooth Italian dessert rested before me, each with a spoon standing at attention in its frozen mass. Frosted with white or dark chocolate and streaks of edible gold, elaborate cakes made of the gelato sat in the refrigerator case to the right. In Newport Beach, even the cakes are upscale.

The mocha gelato seemed to be calling, though the pistachio might be offended. The smooth feel of the mocha in my mouth reminded me of Nora's description regarding her own smooth Italian. Cone in hand, the gelato began melting as I walked up Avocado Street to the office in the warm, California spring. I walked inland and uphill, toward Farallon Street.

Spring could be foggy and gloomy in Newport Beach, but today the fog had burned off early—warming the grass, cement and air. For a moment I walked backward up the hill, calves burning with the steep climb up Avocado. I breathed in the smell of mown lawns and exhaust fumes.

Glare from the ocean felt like lightning on my retinas. I had to shade my face as I looked out over the azure line to Catalina Island. On the rare days the smog and fog didn't obscure my sight of Catalina, I couldn't stop humming the tune "Twenty-Six Miles Across the Sea," which then stayed in my head all day.

Today I sucked in the whole ocean view, dotted with sailing vessels, and turned facing uphill to climb. I could just begin to feel the sweat trickle between my breasts—so much for the crisp tan linen suit. I would soon look like I had been Sumo wrestling during lunch.

Nearing my destination, I sought intermittent shade from the ficus trees lining the street on one side. When I arrived at the intersection of Farallon and Avocado, there was my door on the building labeled "Newport Art Theft Detail." I can't help it, but I always feel proud to see that. There are only two full-time art theft details in the United States, one being in Los Angeles under the aegis of the LAPD, and the other one is our Orange County equivalent.

The tan building was stucco above and below, with windows sandwiched between. Windows surrounded three sides of the building, offering a view of the trees outside and the ocean beyond. How the Art Theft Detail had managed to snag such prime real estate was a mystery, but the location was near a number of museums and galleries. This often kept work nearby and I never failed to be impressed with the view.

Inside the building was less grand. Stained and faded gray carpet lay beneath a series of gray fabric cubicles composed of half walls. I could just make out the series of brunette, blond and gray haired heads of co-workers over the half walls of the cubicles. Sometimes I wondered if a wig on a stand in my cubicle might allow me a brief vacation.

I caught sight of Artie—my partner—who sat in the cubicle across from mine, leaning on his chin and scrolling down the computer screen checking his favorite website: Interpol. A protein bar sat unattended between his lips.

Artie was really Detective Arthur Grey, but no one called him that. He did introduce himself as Arthur though, because "Artie the Art Detective" was just a bit too much and brought on old, tired jokes Artie despised.

"Interpol again, Artie? Find anything juicy today? I don't suppose you found anything on that Qing dynasty ruyi scepter we're supposed to recover, did you?" I picked up a manila folder full of "A" priority files on my desk and threw them onto the "B" pile. There had been no change in their status over lunch, but it made me feel better.

I had once read in a women's magazine in an airport that it was recommended for workers to keep A, B and C file folders on their desks. This would help them better manage their days. The advice was about as useful as that from the same magazine explaining how women can make their lipstick last all day or how to whiten their teeth while gardening.

Artie pulled the protein bar out of his mouth and moved the flat screen to the side for me to see. "No, I have no clue where the scepter is, but this is kind of interesting. Take a look."

"What is it?" I didn't bother to look up. I was too busy shoving my purse under the chair with my foot. I ran my tongue over my teeth, trying to decide if I wanted to squander the time to find a toothbrush in my desk.

He paraphrased from the Interpol website, "It's a tapestry. Interpol just posted it today. It was reported stolen by the Vatican. It's a sixteenth-century Flemish work housed for 500 years or so in the Vatican, but now the Pope is short one tapestry." He looked to me for comment.

I collapsed my face in faux misery, "Oh, how sad that is for His Excellency. So this tapestry is nearly as old as the Pope himself?" I loved to expend sarcasm on the Pope, probably because the topic had been so sacred in school. Papal age and infallibility were among my favorite targets in my ancient Catholic education.

Artie feigned shock and disappointment at my lack of

respect. "Oh my, you're speaking of His Holiness. There should be more reverence in your voice. You should at least show some enthusiasm that the tapestry was 'liberated' from the Vatican."

He was leaning back in the gray chair now. The protein bar had been partially consumed, and he was talking with a bit of a cheek pouch. The cheek pouch was *de rigeur* for Artie. He seemed to eat all the time but was thin and muscular. He was only a few inches taller than me, and lied about his height by stretching it to 5 feet 10 inches when I think it was closer to 5 feet 8 inches—but no matter.

"Sorry," I said. "It was probably a racy scene, so the Vatican had it stolen to spare the cardinals from another night of self-flagellation." I couldn't help myself. Artie was the perfect foil for this kind of thing. We could do this all day, and frequently did.

I loved Artie in the only way one can love a partner. I could say anything to him. Absolutely anything. He'd give an opinion without judgment attached. I would say he was a father figure, but he wasn't that much older and—unlike my father—was completely non-judgmental. It was wonderful. He always had his facts at hand, presenting them without investment like a lobster salad from an indifferent waiter— either you liked lobster or you didn't.

I leaned over Artie's shoulder and pointed to the screen. "Actually, that's quite beautiful." I perused the Interpol description of the stolen item while he read aloud.

"So it's three meters wide and two and a half meters tall, with gold and silver threads, no doubt long since tarnished," he interjected, "and depicts a scene of an enclosed garden with animals in the center. The background is a mille-fleur design." He pronounced it 'mealfloor' and made a broken wrist motion, "...with a border of various floral and religious symbols, blah blah blah..." Artie finished, looking up. "How long is a meter?"

I said I thought a meter was about three feet or so. "Gold or silver threads, huh?" I was impressed. "That must have been commissioned by a king, queen or pope. Popes had plenty of money back then as well. Sometimes they even had girlfriends too. And boyfriends, let's not forget boyfriends." I really couldn't resist.

He clicked off the Interpol site. "Yeah, I've heard it all from you before. Well, a tapestry from the Vatican isn't likely to surface in Newport Beach, is it?" He turned to his desk and placed an orange peel I hadn't noticed before on top of a stack of manila folders. "Are you ready to meet with the chief, now that your two-hour lunch is over?

My heartbeat picked up and my ears felt hot. It was time to face Simon Bayles for a daily review of cases. As usual Artie would pretend not to notice my disquietude, but he was up-to-date on my heartbroken condition. I didn't act like a love-sick teenager and I didn't pace or whine. At least I could be proud of that. However, I couldn't calm my pounding heart.

Chapter Four

Beatrice in 1519

The two men who came into the tapisserie in the Year of Our Lord 1519 were Father Bernardo and an agent to Duke Giulio Campezzi. My Father was accustomed to working with agents of wealthy, Italian patrons. Marie and I sat quietly during Father's negotiations. Father Bernardo was new to Bruges. My Father knew of him, but Marie and I had never met him.

I eyed both men as Father wrote down the dimensions of the work the agent was commissioning. My Father was tall with a fine head of hair—graying in the front—usually covered by a handsome, wool cap. I admired Father's straight nose and deep voice, but most of all I loved my Father's great arms. With strong arms and a low voice, I convinced myself he was the human version of a tree and could stand against any storm. He had been Mother's tree and now he was my tree.

Father Bernardo—on the other hand—was uninteresting, short and sweaty. Why he was here was a mystery. He held himself as was common with the office of priest: high chin and a nose above the rest of us. I thought he smelled a bit like cat piss, and I whispered this to Marie who had to turn to face the wall to prevent our guests from seeing her face as it collapsed in laughter. Mother would have beaten my bottom for saying "cat piss," but she was gone now.

The agent of the Duke was grandly dressed and spoke with a melodic voice. Father informed the agent of his own plans for the textile. The tapestry was to be about two and a quarter ells by three and one-half ells. Father explained that the ell was the length from the tip of the middle finger to the end of the elbow.

The agent went on to affirm that the Duke would want silver and gold thread. Father nodded, repeating, "Of course, of course," though I knew verdure tapestries seldom had silver or gold threads—such effrontery from these wealthy patrons and their agents, to tell a master his craft.

Father mentioned other colors he thought should be used while picking up several of the shuttles my sister and I had placed in baskets to demonstrate to the Duke's agent. Marie and I loved the baskets of colored wool so carefully hand dyed. The reds were the most precious, because they were dyed with crushed insect bodies or from *madder*: a crushed plant. The blues were dyed in urine and woad. Yellows were treated with fustic. All of the hues available were presented in baskets to the agent.

The work was to be an enclosed garden with animals. Father suggested several animals, while being careful by avoiding recommending any that might symbolize evil. He encouraged the Duke's agent to consider a floral background—a mille-fleur—and then they began to talk about prices and timetables. The agent was adamant that the piece be finished in time for the Duke to travel with it to the Vatican, where he was to be married by Pope Leo X of the de' Medici family. The Duke would bring the tapestry with him on his travels as a gift to his wife.

As the negotiation progressed, I noticed something that made me watch with trepidation. Father Bernardo was looking, no, staring at Marie. He moved toward her as the agent discussed fees with my Father. The priest had a red face with greasy hair that fell below his ears. His nose was bulbous and greasy. I identified the smell this time. It was like the pile of vegetable scrapings behind our house.

"What is your name, child?" he asked Marie. His eyes were locked on the neckline of her dress. His head was sweating on top where the slimy hair adhered to the scalp, covered in patches with pink scales and white at their edges. There was dried white spittle collected at the corners of his mouth, and he seemed to wheeze from his excessive girth.

My sister glanced down, quickly adjusting her bodice. Would the priest think we should not be here? Would he believe we were to be home, occupied with the tasks appropriate for young girls of decent families? Would he reprimand us and send us home?

Marie and I did not like the boredom of embroidery. We preferred the organized chaos of the tapisserie. However, we were two girls among twelve men, and perhaps our presence would be forbidden by the church. The guilds allowed us to be there, but the church was more powerful than the guilds.

"Marie" she answered him, eyes still cast to the floor. He put his hand under her chin to lift her face.

Should he be touching her?

"How old are you Marie?"

"Fifteen, Father. My sister, Beatrice, is fourteen," she pointed to me. His eyes remained locked on her.

"I will come to you tomorrow. I have not seen you or your sister at church. I will hear your confession at your home."

He left abruptly, but I felt his dark eyes slide over me like the feeling of dead eels piled in a fish basket.

CHAPTER FIVE

Nora's Party

The evening was cool and breezy with the promise of being downright chilly later, like most coastal evenings in Newport Beach. I suspected I should have brought a shawl to go along with the black dress when I stepped out of the car on Ptarmigan Drive. Stars were hidden behind dense evening fog, which kept those of us living on the coast wondering if the Milky Way had fallen from the sky. I remembered the Milky Way vaguely from my youth, but the coast of California was no way to view it these days—I heard that the outback of Australia still sported a nice view.

The smell of the ocean was clean, and I felt that this evening would be about renewal. Nora was right. It was time to depart the Simon love train. My meeting with him today convinced me again that it was time to "let go" as they say in the self-help books. Detach. Okay. As soon as I figured out how to do that, it would be done. Hear me roar.

I headed up the drive to Paolo's house. Like many houses in Newport Beach, it was perched on a steep drive and the ocean-facing walls were all glass. I couldn't imagine how they might survive an earthquake, not an unknown occurrence on this side of the San Andreas Fault.

I rang the bell. Nora answered, entwined in a man's arm. "Come in!" She pulled me inside, enclosing me in an enthusiastic hug.

Nora's ensemble this evening included tight black cropped pants, black stiletto sandals, and a low-cut silk blouse in a zebra print. Tonight Nora was prey, not predator. I assumed that the arm around Nora's waist was Paolo's arm.

"Claire, this is Paolo Campezzi. Paolo, this is my dear friend, Claire DeMaer." Nora pulled us in close, but I stepped back to allow greater social space. I'm reserved, even slightly suspicious, with people I don't know well.

My reserve has always been confused with contempt or arrogance. It played havoc with my college love-life. At parties I would find myself backing up gradually to increase the distance from a drunken frat boy coming on to me, only to find that I had backed myself into a corner—literally. Men I found attractive would questioningly accuse me, "Why are you so angry?" when I was pensive or anxious. I just had one of those faces for which smiling seemed foreign and feigned to onlookers.

Paolo was slightly taller than Nora. He was wearing a cashmere, black sweater with pumpkin-colored, silk trousers that fell in perfect folds over a flat stomach. I noticed buttery soft, Italian loafers worn without socks in the same pumpkin color. *Who wears pumpkin?* The answer? Nora's latest squeeze—with a cleft chin and a glass house on a cliff.

He did have great hair, just as Nora had mentioned.

Paolo had dark, blond hair that was longish and the kind of unshaven look that had taken over Hollywood recently—unlike Simon's short, dark curls. There was a playful, slightly dangerous look; a look Nora seemed to love about him. I hoped the dangerous part was only her imagination.

Paolo leaned over my hand, while keeping his eyes—deep brown—glued to my modest décolletage. He bent to kiss the hand I tried to extend for a handshake. "It's a very great pleasure. Nora has spoken of you quite often." Charm, charm, charm, thy name is Paolo.

His hands were soft and his accent as buttery as the shoes. I had no problem imagining Paolo in a steamy Italian movie. For shame. I felt the buzz of crimson in my face and neck, and smiled broadly in goofy discomfort.

Bowing slightly to both of us, Paolo let go of my hand and turned to Nora. "I need to make sure that the crostini are not burning, my love. I will find you in a few minutes. Claire, please enjoy the house tour." He turned into the foyer, entering the crowd. I let out a breath, unaware I had been holding it.

As we moved inside the door, I glanced at Nora's neck above the zebra print. "Nora, are those teeth you have around your neck?" I moved in closer to point at the necklace.

"Do you like them? They're shark's teeth."

"Oh, shark's teeth." God love her.

Nora pointed to the floor in the entryway. "This is the Brazilian mahogany floor with onyx inlay I was telling you about. I worked on this for months, but I like the way it turned out, don't you?"

I nodded in assent, but Nora was already moving on to

compliment herself on the next design coup. An onyx floor. The cost of the floor probably exceeded my yearly income. What was onyx? It sounded like an animal from the African veldt—no, that was oryx.

We walked past a huge, circular table of wrought-iron topped with stone. A hotel-lobby-sized Hawaiian floral arrangement spilled forth from a bronze vase.

Stepping down, we entered a large living space with a 180-degree ocean view. There was a stone fireplace on the side opposite the ocean view with an ornately carved wooden mantle, the wood extending to a 30-foot ceiling. A gilded mirror rested atop the mantle in the new style, with the mirror leaning against the wall. I speculated that Paolo couldn't afford the large nail to hang the mirror on the wall after paying Nora's design fee.

I could see Nora's influence everywhere. Though she dressed like a gun moll, her design work was opulent and tasteful to those who experienced it. She leaned toward earthy colors: deep reds, warm bittersweet chocolates, bronzes and gold.

Perusing decorator items with Nora was a favorite activity. Nora would ask my opinion and, when given it, would answer, "What do you know? You're a detective for pity sake."

Nora pointed at the wine and refreshments held by a waiter, "Sparkling water with lime?" She knew this was my drink of choice. In a past life I had been wedded to alcohol, but there had been a bitter divorce.

"Works for me," I took one from a waiter with wet-looking hair while taking note of the guests in the room.

The men tended to have slick hair. I made a mental note to purchase hair gel stock from my broker. Oh, right, I didn't have a broker.

"You look good tonight." Nora leaned in to whisper. "I can actually see a little T&A in that dress. Was that a mistake?"

"Probably," I pulled simultaneously at my hem and held on to the bodice. I sipped the sparkling water and gestured out to the room. "The place is amazing, Nora. You've outdone yourself."

Nora turned around in place with her arms spread, looking like the opening scene of *The Sound of Music* if one replaced the nun's habit with tight faux zebra. "I know! Come see the library next."

The floor of the library was covered in a plush wool carpet the color of cayenne pepper. Bookcases of burled wood extended from floor to ceiling on all walls except for one. The books were leather-bound and smelled new. Nora moved her arm toward a large wall without bookshelves. "This is the *pièce de résistance!*" She pointed to the wall opposite us. On it was a faded mille-fleur tapestry in green, blue, brown, gold and pink, with tarnished silver threads.

Chapter Six

Beatrice's Concerns 1519

ather Bernardo was to be in our home while we were unattended? I could not believe what I had heard. Was my Father aware of this? He would never allow a man to enter our home while he was away at the tapisserie, and what did Marie have to confess?

When the two men left I ran to Marie and tugged on her long sleeve. "He has an unbecoming countenance," I whispered. "And why did he touch you? Did you see his head? What are those scaly patches? Does he have the pox?"

Marie answered as a wiser sister would, "He is a priest, Beatrice. Do not be vexed. His work is difficult, but it is the work of God. His kind offer is to be graciously accepted."

I told Father I did not like or trust the priest, but he was still locked within the fog of his grief and distraction of a new and important commission. He waved me away as he answered without looking at my face, "Beatrice, you are a suspicious child. He is a man of God. If you cannot trust a man of God, whom can you trust?"

CHAPTER SEVEN

Claire Sees the Unexpected

My drink stopped at the edge of my lips. I felt as if someone had just poured the thing down the back of my tiny black dress.

"Have you ever seen anything like this before?" Nora smiled and looked to me for confirmation. Confidence in her design sense had given her a smirk of self-satisfaction.

I hesitated. There were the animals in the enclosed garden surrounded by the mille-fleur background. My hands became slippery with sweat as I searched for words. I licked lips that seemed stuck to my teeth. Nora nudged my arm. "Yes, I believe I have," I said, never taking my eyes from the stolen Interpol tapestry.

I said nothing to Nora or Paolo about the tapestry. Around nine I made excuses over Nora's objections and left. My concerns over meeting strangers and making small talk had abated, as I became obsessed with the catastrophe in the library.

I drove home along Pacific Coast Highway, abbreviated by

locals as PCH, listening to the ocean waves crashing onto the rocks—or maybe it was the sound of my heart pounding once again. I wasn't sure.

I made a turn onto Dahlia Street in Corona del Mar and wound my way to Begonia. Though the bungalows had charming gardens to identify their owners, at night they all looked alike.

I pulled my gold 1967 Mustang under the garage loft apartment, got out and locked the garage door. Usually this place felt like home. Today it felt cold and dark.

Nora and I found this apartment while walking one day behind a troop of jogging Marines who were wearing tiny loden-colored shorts. They sang in unison, "I don't know but I've been told, streets of heaven are paved with gold." We followed them for quite a while watching their bodies move in unison when I spotted the apartment.

It was a few blocks from the ocean. My affordable loft was tucked behind the bungalow, over the garage. If I stretched out and crawled through the bathroom window there was a 4-foot opening onto the flat roof and an ocean view—though I had to sit on the gravel roof to enjoy it. My beagle, Leila, and I had tried to sit out on the roof, but the gravel was too hot and uncomfortable so we ditched the idea of sunning on the roof.

I walked out of the garage and pulled open a wooden gate, covered with ivy, making the short walk to the entry staircase. I could hear Leila whine and paw at the door. Normally Leila stayed in the fenced backyard, but tonight she was inside.

I assumed Maizie, the landlord's 13 year-old daughter

who took Leila for walks and fed her every day, had put her inside. Maizie and Leila had been buddies since I had brought the puppy home. Maizie had grabbed the then 7-week old Leila's velvety ears while Leila rolled onto her back, legs pawing wildly in the air with her pink, freckled belly exposed. That was several years ago, and Maizie and Leila had fallen into a comfortable arrangement. Maizie did everything for Leila, and Leila slept on Maizie's feet while she did homework. Occasionally Leila would deign to accept a dog treat from Maizie. The dog insisted on running under a bush to eat it, in case Maizie felt inclined to down the thing herself.

I worked out a payment arrangement of sorts with Maizie for giving care to the dog. Dinners, movies and various treats were involved—but mostly the payments consisted of me teaching Maizie kick-boxing. I had once been required to braid ribbons into Maizie's hair for a school play, but even she could see that the result was like something out of Greek mythology rather than being hip. I had short wavy hair so Maizie's mane was puzzling and overwhelming to me.

Leila had a cozy house outside as well as in under the section of the garage underneath my staircase. She could spend each day sunning in the backyard or playing with the landlady's uppity cat named Portia.

I unlocked the door, catching Leila's collar before she could escape into the yard. She rolled onto her back, and I bent over to rub her belly. Too tired and upset to climb the stairs, I sat on the bottom step petting the silken ears and shaking my head in disbelief.

Finally, I took to the stairs like an octogenarian shouldering wet cement.

I threw my keys on a small, dark, red oriental table under two oddly placed hexagonal windows. Nora had called the windows "unexpected." I thought they made the place look like a dismal chapel or the dressing room of a televangelist.

Leila's toenails clicked on the slate floor. The apartment felt very cold. I adjusted the heat. In antique Californian apartments positioned over garages there are small wall heaters, looking like Frigidaires, cut in half lengthwise and glued to the wall. The heaters are wholly inefficient for heating two levels as only the top level, the loft where the bed is located, would be able to get toasty in a matter of minutes. However, I wasn't sure I would get warm whether I was upstairs or downstairs. I felt cold in my soul.

On most days, this was my haven. I recalled Nora yammering about the required paint colors, all with spicy names. Nora insisted the dark red on the staircase was "paprika" with "mustard yellow" on the walls of the living space. The couch was sage green, and a Persian rug repeated the colors.

Everything reminded me of Nora and our friendship—every pillow and lamp.

During shopping trips for the apartment my hands had gone to plain, beige paint and upholstery. Nora would make a face, as if she'd stepped barefoot on a banana slug, pronouncing, "Your personality is beige! You can't live in a beige apartment!"

Tonight even the warm glow from the small lamp on the desk under the loft staircase failed to bring its usual cheer. Next to the lamp was a picture of the two of us, sporting fake black glasses, Groucho noses and toothy smiles. Ah friendship. It was times like these that I could understand the Nigerian proverb, "Hold a true friend with both hands."

I slumped onto the couch, pulling a pillow onto my chest and crushing another under my head. I rubbed my eyes until those little dots appeared behind the lids. Leila padded up the second set of stairs to the loft, waiting for me to follow.

I stared at the ceiling. Leila's tail drummed rhythmically on the floor. This was her invitation for me to come up to bed.

What on earth was I going to do about the tapestry? Maybe I could do nothing. That might work.

Leila padded back down to the living room, ears low, and tried a dismal tail thump for attention. I rose to pace, but Leila remained inert. She'd seen the pacing before.

Maybe I was mistaken about the whole thing. I turned the computer on and logged onto the Interpol site. The tapestry on the screen glowed back at me, damning my do-nothing plan. I leaned back in the computer chair and rubbed my eyes again, moaned loudly, and gradually increased the intensity of the moan while pulling at my hair.

"Leila, what am I going to do?" The dog lowered her head, but the tail thumped harder. She padded to the computer area where I put my head on the keyboard, the letters flying wildly across the screen—*jkl;jkl;jkl;jkl;jkl;*. She nudged my dangling fingers—a doggie gesture of hopeful apology and commiseration.

Chapter Eight

Marie's Confession

Father Bernardo knocked on our door the next day. "I spoke with your sister yesterday. I am Father Bernardo," he said to me as I peered out the door.

The winter air was frigid and damp. Today the brown and frozen canals smelled particularly foul as I opened the door to let him in. I saw fallen fragments of leaves spin on their icy surface.

"You are Beatrice, yes?" He repeated his introduction and looked past me, into the room beyond.

I had been reading Greek mythology and was annoyed at the interruption, especially by this man, whom I neither knew nor trusted. He was not like other priests I had known. I felt uneasy allowing him to enter but it would be unseemly to be rude. Bringing my sister into the room felt like entrusting a jewel to a known thief.

Father Bernardo walked past me and strode to the fireplace. He handed me his cloak and walked into the room before I had granted permission—words of refusal died on my lips. He pulled off his gloves. "I will hear your sister's confession today and come to you next week. Please show me the way, Beatrice. Is your father at home?"

He moved as if he owned our little rooms. I spoke to the back of his head.

"No," I said. "But he will be here soon," I lied. Father never came home mid-day. In fact, today he was in Antwerp. Marie and I were never home at this time, for our work was at the factory. However, we had stayed here only for Father Bernardo to hear Marie's confession, though what a 15-year old girl would have to confess that warranted a house visit by Father Bernardo was an enigma. My sister accompanied me every day at the factory. Our lives were intertwined and I knew of no heinous sins, beyond that of Original Sin, the stain we all bore.

I led Father Bernardo through our sitting room, hung with some of Father's earliest tapestries, to Father's study. Marie and I seldom used that room because Father read and wrote correspondences there, but I lit a fire so Marie would not be cold.

"Thank you Beatrice. That will be all," he said as Marie entered. Why did Father Bernardo not wish to hear my confession today as well? He closed the heavy door as I was about to protest, but one does not protest to a priest.

I went back to my reading while Father Bernardo was with Marie. I lost myself while reading my favorite myths, including the myth of Philomela. Though from time to time I heard muffled sounds, I assumed Marie was speaking or praying. When I looked up the pungent priest was in the doorway.

"Beatrice, you are reading, I see." His voice seemed too loud for the small room and his face looked sweaty again. He smelled of animal odors. "It is not God's desire that girls be taught to read," he said and pointed to my book.

Heat seared into my cheeks. "Does God speak to you of his desires, Father Bernardo?"

I could hardly believe my impertinence. As soon as the words left my lips I knew I had made a terrible error. The Church was powerful and he surely was not to be trusted. His lips were thick, puffy and red. The day was cold, yet he was red and sweating. His chest was heaving, no doubt with anger at my audacity.

"Forgive me, Father Bernardo," I said quickly staring at the floor. I swallowed hard. "I only mean that it is a source of amazement and wonder that God speaks to you of His desires as He would never speak to a maiden. You are most surely blessed."

The groveling seemed to appease him. However, I felt revolted by my weakness, and loathed him all the more for pushing me to it.

His booming voice filled the room as gloves were pulled over his corpulent wrists. "I am fortunate to be made the agent of the Lord our God. I must talk to your father about your habits, Beatrice. Perhaps he does not understand how much time a young woman needs to spend in prayer for the sin of being born to tempt the sons of Adam. Nevertheless, I understand your mother is no longer with us on this Earth to show you girls how to live in the image of the Blessed Virgin. God bless you Beatrice."

He made the sign of the cross over me and pulled open the heavy wooden door to exit.

He left and then I closed the door tightly, putting my back against it. I turned to lock it. I did not scream or pound on the door. I felt cold, very cold, and my breath could not be stilled. How dare he speak of our mother when he did not know her!

I moved across the room and opened the study door. Marie was on the floor! She sat face down with her hand covering her head as if something had fallen and struck her from above.

"Marie, what has happened? Are you all right? Why are you on the floor?" I ran to her. Her skirt was torn and her tied-on sleeves fell to her elbows. She was wearing her best flax skirt. It was tattered and hanging as limp as a dead bird on a fence.

"Marie, did you know your dress was torn...?" She looked up before I finished. She began to rock back and forth, pulling the torn silk from her underskirt in strips. Without looking at me, she spoke so quietly that I had to put my ear next to her lips to hear her say, "Beatrice, you must never tell Father."

"Never tell Father what?" Marie's lip was bleeding. Her undergarments were visible. "Marie, your clothes are a sight. What has happened?" I put my hand gently over her hands to prevent her from tearing the silk.

While rocking she repeated, "You must never tell Father."

CHAPTER NINE

Claire's Conundrum

I pointed to the Interpol website and the tapestry. Artie's mouth was open. "It was hanging in his library?" he asked, the half-eaten protein bar stopping mid-air.

"Yes, unfortunately," I paced behind his chair. My head itched and I ran fingers through my hair while looking at the gray floor for an answer to rise up from it.

"What do you mean unfortunately? Hey! You've just broken an international case. What could be better? Are you nuts?" Artie's expression was triumphant. He took a bite of the bar.

"Look, it's complicated. Paolo is Nora's boyfriend, her lover. *Nora*. You know, Nora, my best friend. She's in love with him."

"Okay, so it's complicated. But, I don't see that you have a choice. You have to turn him over to the Vatican authorities. What did Simon say?"

"I haven't spoken with Simon about it yet. Let's go over to Paolo's place first. Maybe there's a reasonable explanation for why he has a tapestry stolen from the Vatican." I saw the look of puzzlement and incredulity on Artie's face.

He watched me negotiate the small space between desks. He took a long pull at his paper coffee cup before setting down on a stained stack of manila files, nodding. "Oh, I'm sure there is."

"Come on Artie. Do it with me now. I can't stand this. Will you get the car?"

He threw the bar wrapper and coffee cup in the trash and mumbled something while pulling the car keys from his pocket. His laptop closed with a louder-than-necessary slam.

Artie brought his car to the front of the building. Today was hotter than yesterday, and the metal surface shimmered with reflected heat. When I entered the car I pulled myself carefully onto the hot leather seat, lifting my thighs off the leather. I felt the heat through my linen suit.

We pulled out onto Avocado heading toward the ocean and PCH.

I reviewed mentally, *Hi Nora, I'm here to arrest your lover.* No. *Hi Nora, does Paolo have an arrest record?* No again. *Hey Nora, how much do you trust Paolo?*

The drive to Paolo's took longer than expected because of heavy traffic moving both directions on PCH. We crept from light to light while I stared at rug shops and espresso bars. I struck the dashboard with both palms. "Jeez, these must be the worst drivers in the world!"

Artie glanced my way, raising a brow. "A little anxious are we, DeMaer?" Hippie beads swung incongruously with a pendulum motion from the rearview mirror. The beads were the only sound in the car.

I asked him once what were with the beads, as they were

not exactly his style. He had smiled in a wistful way, touching the beads softly. "Belonged to someone I loved," was all he said.

It was too creepy to think that Artie actually had a hippie lover at some time in the past or a lover anytime, anywhere. I preferred to think of Artie as a neutered, neutral gender, non-sexual being. It was inconceivable that Artie could have had a lover or ever engage in sex—too messy for Artie. What would he do with his protein bar during sex?

By the time we reached the house twenty minutes later, I hoped Nora was out shopping for more ossified jewelry. We left the air-conditioned car and met the hazy heat reflected off Paolo's driveway, as we walked to the front door.

I put my hand out to ring the bell of Paolo's home, but my fingers couldn't quite receive the brain command to do so.

Artie pushed my finger down on the button hard. As he looked at the exterior of the home, I heard him grumble, "... guy must be loaded."

Paolo answered the door with Nora at his side. I shot Artie a desperate glance, but he missed it intentionally. *Damn Artie. Terrible partner. Just you wait.*

Today Paolo wore cream-colored linen pants and a silk, khaki T-shirt. The man had style. It would be useless to him in prison.

Paolo didn't appear to remember me, but Nora shrieked, "Claire! Hey, come in. What a nice surprise. Hi Artie! Did you call to say you were coming? I didn't listen to our messages yet today. The place is really messy, but the party was a success!"

Nora's blonde hair was piled into an alligator clip on top

of her head, and she wore fur slippers that matched a fur-trimmed robe.

"Paolo, this is Claire's partner, Detective Arthur Grey, but we call him Artie if he's being a good boy." There was a conspiratorial wink. Artie flushed around the collar and suddenly found his shoes fascinating. He and Nora played this game frequently, but Nora was the hands-down winner every time.

"My pleasure," Paolo said and extended a hand to Artie. He bowed his head slightly to me. "Nora and I were going over some cabinet plans for the upstairs bath. Won't you come in?"

He ushered us through the foyer where we could see the detritus from the night before. Wine glasses had been washed, but sat in open cardboard boxes for the caterer to retrieve. Serving trays had cleared platters, but all were stacked on the floor in various parts of the room.

Artie's eyes roamed the entryway. I knew he wasn't missing a thing.

Artie had forgotten more than I'd ever know about art theft. Also, he had incredible observational and listening skills. He didn't fill air time with his own voice. When people spoke, he would watch their faces and body language. He could write down notes after a conversation with perfect recall.

"I thought last night went very well," Nora spoke as Paolo looked at her, and both smiled. Nora touched his unshaven face lightly.

This was going to be very painful. Why did I go to that ridiculous party? I could have stayed home to re-read *Middlemarch*.

"Everyone loved Nora's work, but then who wouldn't?" Paolo said. "Nora is very talented and beautiful—but you already know that, Claire. I understand you two have been friends for years." Paolo pulled Nora in to him and gave her a kiss that landed just north of her mouth. He pulled at the ties of her robe.

Art cleared his throat. *Damn shitty partner. I would transfer out of the detail this afternoon.*

Paolo gestured us toward the kitchen. "May I offer you something to drink? I'm having a tonic with lime. May I get one for you? Nora and I are sitting in the kitchen."

A wide expanse of black granite loomed before them. I had not been in the kitchen the night before. Artie and I both declined a drink.

"I'll take one, darling," said Nora. Nora looked radiantly happy. I wished I sold insurance for a living.

"Mr. Campezzi..." I began. Already I felt stupid and awkward. Why wasn't Artie doing the talking? *Coward.*

Paolo stopped me with a wagging finger, "No, you must call me Paolo." He should wipe that cheerful smile off his face.

I started again. Shitty air quality made my throat tight. It was the worst part about living in Southern California. Well, the second worst. The traffic was the worst. No, the expense...what the hell, I was moving to Canada anyway.

I rubbed my eyes, stalling for time. I thought of those bug zappers, the ones where the bug is flying about with no cares and *fzzt!* Incineration. My friendship with Nora—*fzzt!*

I pulled my shoulders back. "I'm afraid that Mr. Grey and I are here on business, rather than pleasure, Mr. Campezzi."

Paolo squeezed the lime into a tall glass and poured the tonic over the ice. The black granite reflected the light from the windows. There was an ocean view from the kitchen. The man really appeared to have it all and was about to lose everything.

He took a drink before asking, "What kind of business?" He smiled and leaned his backside against the granite, one hand resting at its beveled edge and the other holding his drink. Nora looked up from the cabinet samples strewn before her on the kitchen table and flashed what appeared to be an adoring, albeit confused, smile at Paolo.

"Mr. Campezzi, I don't know if you remember from the introductions last night, but I work with the Newport Art Theft Detail. Mr. Grey is my partner. We are here to speak with you about the tapestry in your library."

"Art theft detail—are you concerned that Nora will steal my tapestry?" Paolo smiled subversively at Nora. "Nora, you know what happens to naughty girls!"

"Oh!" Nora squealed in mock terror—as if this was a game.

"No, Mr. Campezzi, I'm concerned that the tapestry has already been stolen."

Chapter Ten

Confession's Consequences

As the weeks passed and the weather warmed, Marie stopped going with me to the tapisserie. She stayed home, keeping to her bed. She rarely spoke and failed to eat her soup in the evenings. She vomited in the mornings. I missed her and asked when she would return, but she gave no reply. Father continued to travel to Antwerp, but when he returned he wondered aloud why Marie did not go to the shop.

One day Marie looked straight into my face and said, "Beatrice, I am with child. I will not return to the tapisserie. You must help me find a place to go. If I am seen with my growing belly I will be cast out...or worse."

She took me by the hand and pulled my hand to her lips, covering it with kisses while whispering, "Help me." Her voice was small. She put her head on my shoulder and I felt the quiet, desperate shaking of her shoulders.

I tried to speak, patting my hand on her linen cap, whispering words I do not remember. I felt her hopelessness.

I knew nothing of babies or how they were made. Mother had never spoken of it, and Father would not be the one to ask such things. Marie and I had talked about the subject many times, but what we had seen the farm animals do—surely it must be different with men and women.

"I will help you. What do you want me to do? I do not understand." My beloved Marie was my closest ally, but I was a child. I had no idea how I could help.

Marie told me then what had happened during confession.

Father Bernardo began by asking Marie if she ever had impure thoughts.

Marie thought he was referring to the hateful thoughts she had of Katerina VerBeke. She wanted Katerina to be swallowed up by the earth. Katerina was jealous of Marie and had hurtfully slandered her. Marie confessed, "Yes, I do have impure thoughts." Katerina was a flirt, and she had charmed young Jan.

Father Bernardo stood then and moved toward her. He placed his hand on the skin of her neck. "I knew you did Marie." He stroked her throat. She could see his breathing quicken. "I knew what you were thinking yesterday in your father's shop." His sour breath made Marie turn her head. He pushed her against the wall.

His hand moved down into her bodice and his fingers found her nipple and pinched it hard. "I could see that you wanted me. You wanted me here to kiss and lick your breasts," he panted as he pressed against her. "You wanted to tempt me."

Marie was stunned. Was this penance for impure thoughts? He moved his lips to her nipple and she pushed at his head with the heels of her hands, but they slipped against his greasy pate. His teeth bit into her breast, and he moved his mouth over hers to muffle her voice as she called out "No!" He pressed hard against her mouth until she felt she could not breathe.

Without moving his mouth, Father Bernardo lifted Marie's skirt. She sputtered against his mouth, her spittle on his cheeks. He put a dry finger between her legs. It hurt terribly. Marie pushed away from his hand as hard as she could. He crushed her lips—she tasted blood. She moved her mouth aside to gasp for air.

"Father, please stop. Is this my penance? I am so sorry. Please stop. I cannot breathe." She said it felt as if her chest was being crushed. She feared she would be suffocated. Perhaps suffocation was to be her penance, she thought.

He pulled the finger out and fumbled with his cassock. "You tempted me. You are a temptress. I can match your power. Do you want to see my power?" When he had freed his stiff sex organ he pushed inside her, like a dog in the street. His breath was coming fast now, and there was that fetid smell. "I will route the devil from you. The temptress will be vanquished," he said as he pushed and panted. "I will make you clean by putting the seed of God back into you."

Marie cried and tried to push him away as he thrust and thrust. It hurt terribly. She could feel something wet on her legs. She was mortified. Had she wet herself in fear she wondered?

Marie's head was battered against the stone fireplace as Father Bernardo pushed against her. She felt her head rock back against the stone: knocking and knocking, rocking—floating. She watched herself float and rock, float and rock, float and rock...

She saw herself in a rocking chair. Papa's desk chair was a rocking chair. She was rocking hard, and the sound of her head hitting the wall became the sound of the rocker hitting the desk.

She saw herself as a girl sitting at Papa's desk, her short legs barely able to reach the floor. She was playing with Papa's quills. He would be angry. She was a bad girl and would be punished, like the girl at the fireplace fornicating in Papa's office.

When it was over, Marie readjusted her dress and slumped down the wall onto the floor. Father Bernardo's voice was husky and breathless, "Ah there, my child, I have washed you with the cleansing power of the Lord," he said as he pulled his cassock down over his shrunken, vile member.

"You must never tell anyone of this or you will be burned at the stake for your brush with the devil. I can save you from the devil, but I cannot save you from the ſtake."

He leaned over her on the floor. She ſtared ahead—not daring to meet his eyes. "You believe me, don't you Marie?" he asked as he pulled her quivering chin toward him.

She took a long time to answer. She saw the small girl rock in the rocking chair. That girl was weak, a sinner, a fool—she should not have touched Papa's chair. She turned her face away to ſtare at the floor as she whispered, "Yes, Father Bernardo. I do believe you."

CHAPTER ELEVEN

The Arrest

I studied the effect my words had on Paolo.

"Stolen?" He had stopped laughing and looked ready to move toward the library. "But I was just in the library earlier this morning and it was there." His accent was more noticeable now. He placed the emphasis on the third syllable of library, and "it" was pronounced *eet*. His hands gestured toward the library inviting us all to follow.

Nora had a puzzled, uncomfortable look a person gets after eating cottage cheese and then reading that it expired a week ago.

"No," I put up a hand to keep him in the room, "what I mean, sir, is that it appears that you are in possession of stolen property. That tapestry is posted on Interpol as stolen from the Vatican. Can you tell me how you came to be in possession of it?"

"What?" Nora wasn't smiling. She wasn't looking good at all. She was yelling.

"Claire, have you lost it? Really, did I hear you correctly? Are you asking if Paolo stole his own tapestry? It's been in his family for generations. I told you that before the party."

She pulled furiously at the hair clip that had begun to fall to one side of her head.

Paolo set his glass down slowly. He moved to the kitchen window, his back to all of us. He put his head down, making no sound, and braced his arms against the granite counter.

Nora turned to him. Her voice rose. It had a begging quality. The alligator clip had been wrestled into a position at the side of her head, where the blonde hair was half in, half out of the clip. "Paolo, tell Claire that you brought the tapestry with you from your home in Florence. Tell her about all the other art pieces your family has! Paolo, what's wrong?" she asked as he touched his shoulder.

He looked up from the counter and appeared to take in the ocean view for almost a minute before he turned back to us. He licked dry lips and then cleared his throat. His hands moved in and out of trouser pockets. He stood for a long while surveying the kitchen. The cool, Mediterranean pose was gone.

"*Cara mía*—I can explain," he said, his accent thicker than moments earlier. "This might take some time. Will you sit?" He gestured to a kitchen chair. It was covered in a black and beige harlequin pattern I knew Nora had chosen and loved. She had poured out her affection for him into her elegant designs.

Nora ignored Paolo's request and continued to stand. She looked from me, to Paolo, and back again. My suit was stuck to my back and armpits. The ocean-reflection light coming through the kitchen cast unattractive shadows below Paolo's eyes. I saw Nora push at the clip in her disheveled hair.

"The tapestry in my library *is* stolen," Paolo said, at last, words rushing out. There it was.

Nora turned a stricken look on him. "What? What are you saying?"

Artie glanced at me. He must have thought this was going to be very easy. Nora began to pace. Her hair had now fallen down her back in a straggling tangle, with the alligator clip hanging precariously off the bottom.

Paolo picked up where he had left off. "The tapestry was stolen by the Vatican from my family in the sixteenth century. The Vatican has had the tapestry for almost 500 years."

I thought I must have missed something. "I'm sorry Mr. Campezzi, did you say it was stolen *by* the Vatican?"

"Yes. My family has lived in Florence for 500 years. Sometime around 1519 or so, Giulio Campezzi—my ancestor—commissioned a tapestry in Bruges by a master weaver named Cornelius van Hecke. The tapestry was a very important work. The Duke wanted it for his wedding day. He had plans to carry the tapestry with him, as many men of his social stature did on their own travels at the time."

"He was to be married by Pope Leo X. The Duke planned to marry Cecilia Haghenbeek. She was a distant cousin of Margaret of Austria, Aunt to Emperor Charles V. The marriage was planned since they were children, so that the Duke could combine his land with the Haghenbeek business acumen in order to form a grand wine making and distribution business."

Nora traversed the kitchen several times. At some point she had thrown the hair clip in the sink. I followed her agitation while she listened to her lover speak. We were all intensely interested in the details of the provenance.

"The Duke sent an agent to Bruges. This was not unusual. Business was often conducted through an agent. The agent brought money with him as a down-payment on the tapestry. The agent met with Cornelius van Hecke in his factory in Bruges. They agreed upon the size of the work, and for it to be woven with silver and gold thread. You see, the Duke—my ancestor—was very, very wealthy. Or, he would be wealthy with his planned marriage to the Lady Haghenbeek."

Paolo had put down the glass. He rubbed a non-existent spot on the granite. He kept his eyes on the spot as he spoke and rubbed something we couldn't see. Nora moved to the far end of the kitchen where she could stare at him but place herself as far as possible from all of us.

"The tapestry would have taken many months to finish. I don't know how many. It would be delivered by Mr. van Hecke, who would meet Duke Campezzi at some point before the wedding to receive his final payment."

Paolo looked up from the black granite. "This is what was to have taken place, Ms. Claire." He pronounced it *Meez* Claire. "But, you see, it did not." Paolo looked at Nora as he spoke.

"The tapestry was completed, but never delivered. The wedding did not take place. The Duke did not travel to the Vatican."

"For some reason, which no one in my family knows, the Vatican took the tapestry, and the tapestry has been hidden there for almost 500 years. My family has known about this for all this time. We have made many petitions to the Vatican to retrieve the work, but they always denied its existence. Then, last year, I made a trip myself to the Vatican. I knew they were planning an exhibition of their tapestries and hoped they might be foolish enough to put it on display. I was right and they did."

He continued to speak, the Italian accent thick and melodious, like distant jazz music on the sidewalks of New Orleans.

"The exhibition was magnificent. I strolled through the halls and marveled at the incredible works before me. I knew what I was looking for and when I found it I could hardly believe my good fortune. The tapestry was legendary in my family for 500 years. It was time for me to bring it home. I bribed a guard for information about how the tapestries were to be taken down and stored after the exhibition. It was not as difficult as I imagined."

Nora had taken a seat on one of the harlequin kitchen chair cushions, and she began to stare at her rocking foot as Paolo spoke. Her hair hung in pitiable disarray around her face. Mascara blackened large crescents under her eyes.

"I took the tapestry out of the country immediately. I thought it would be safer to bring it to the United States so that it would be forever out of the hands of the Vatican."

With shaking hands, Paolo raised the tonic and lime to his mouth and finished the drink. He fingered the ice in the glass on the kitchen table. Nora stared at the glass. The ice cubes made the only sound in the room as they clinked in the leaded crystal.

He looked at me. "So you see, Ms. DeM...Claire. I did

steal the tapestry, but I also did not. It was my family's to begin with, and I was taking it back after almost 500 years."

Paolo moved across the room and put his hand over Nora's hand. "I'm so sorry, Cara. I thought you would never need to know the story. It is mine. You must believe I am not a thief."

By now his accent was very heavy and his own hair was stuck to his forehead in a limp, sweaty mass. Nora continued to stare at the ice in his glass, her lips pursed.

"So," I cleared my throat, "I assume you have clear documentation of your family's ownership of the tapestry."

"No, I'm afraid I do not. There are no surviving documents pertaining to this tapestry. The only information about it is the oral history that has passed through my family, generation after generation."

Then, as I allowed the words to escape my mouth, the cataclysm: "I'm afraid, Mr. Campezzi, I must place you under arrest. Art, will you read him his rights, please?"

Art crossed the room and began the recitation.

Nora touched me with an ice-cold hand, squeezing hard. "Listen, don't do this." Her voice was shaking. She took a long shuddering breath and wiped her nose with her sleeve.

Nora's voice became a desperate whisper. "You know I'm in love with him. What's the matter with you? Are you so obsessed with that job of yours that you can't see you've made a terrible mistake? Answer me."

I met her eyes and put out a comforting hand. "Nora, he stole it. He took it from the Vatican. He can't prove anything he's saying. It's been in the Vatican holdings for nearly 500 years. When you showed it to me last night I recognized it immediately from the Interpol website. I'm so sorry." Nora pulled her hand away as if mine had spontaneously combusted.

"He needs a good lawyer." I said it, but it sounded pathetic even to me.

"And you need a new best friend." She left the kitchen stifling sobs.

Chapter Twelve

Beatrice Vows Revenge

I cradled Marie in my arms when the story ended. "I will help you," I said as I brushed her warm cheek. She stared ahead, rocking in my arms and whispering low, "I did not mean to do it. I should not have sat in Papa's chair. I did not mean it, Beatrice. I was bad. I am bad. I am a sinner. I will go to hell. God hates me. God hates me. I will never be forgiven." Her hair hung out the back of her linen cap. Her fingers struggled to tear at her cuffs.

My thoughts raced as I vowed that this would be the last confession Father Bernardo would ever hear. What kind of God would allow my sister to suffer thus?

Before our meeting with Father Bernardo I had never questioned faith, God, or religion. These principles I had learned to accept as one does the sunrise each morning or as one recognizes the Church-taught fact that the sun travels around the Earth. Faith, God, and religion were immutable—accepted as an awesome force—sometimes cruel, but only for those who deserved an evil fate. Evil invited evil upon itself. Wicked fates did not befall those of good nature and honest morals, but evil had befallen my sister and my mother as well. These thoughts were incompatible and made my head ache with confusion.

I thought of the meaning of the word *father* as protector and wondered how a protector like Father Bernardo could betray my sister. Would he be struck dead by God? Would Marie? How had this happened—how had we come to trust the Church and its agents to do good or do right by the common man? What made us the common man? It sounded so vulgar, but Father Bernardo was the vulgar one, not my sister. I could not believe that the hand of God would guide Father Bernardo to rape my sister. What kind of God was that?

Weeks went by and Father was due home. By early summer I contacted our old neighbor, Mevrouw DeGroot, at the Begijnhof de Wijngaard behind the Minnewater. The nunnery on the canal had been Mevrouw DeGroot's home since her husband died, and she agreed that the good women there would take in Marie.

I helped Marie pack her belongings into a small bag. It broke my heart to see the small number of treasured items that represented her life. She should be preparing to wed Jan. It was obvious that they could build a life together, and Jan would become the master once Father stopped working at the tapisserie. I thought of the times I had seen Jan brush his hand against hers as she brought woolen thread to refill his basket. Jan was sweet and young, smelling of rosemary. He would have been a kind husband. Marie and I would have shared the quiet delights of romantic gossip.

We should be planning her wedding gown and discussing whether apricot tarts or blueberry would suit the guild guests. I could smell the scents of boughs, cakes and ale mixed with candle wax. These should be the scents surrounding Marie holding the hand of her handsome Jan during the wedding feast, both their faces warm and reddened in the candlelight.

Instead together Marie and I walked without speaking to the Begijnhof. Resting on a hill overlooking the canal, the residence of the Beguine nuns sheltered the compassionate women who aided the sick and poor. In the distance we heard troubadours playing the music of Josquin de Prez. We used to love his music and would crowd into the square to hear his works played, but now it was a background dirge.

Walking as men to the gallows, the solace of the beautiful refuge was lost on us. The quiet nunnery had been here for over 275 years offering meditation for the nuns and their guests—as my sister would now be.

We passed willows dipping their water-laden tips into a calm pool, reflected there like green lace. White swans swam beneath the overhanging branches, their reflections a puddle of wavy white beneath them, with cygnets on their backs.

The swans were incredibly special to Bruges and, in

times of joy before this, Marie and I would visit them. A hundred years or so earlier, the people of Bruges pledged to care for the swans forever in order to atone for the execution of a servant to Maximilian of Austria. Their beaks were marked with a "B" to identify their home in Bruges.

The nuns of the Begijnhof walked quietly under the dappled shade of the trees. Their large, white starched wimples bounced softly with their footfalls, and their hands were hidden in ample sleeves. Their serenity was juxtaposed against my racing thoughts of how to save Marie.

We walked past stone buildings with small-paned windows, the stone mottled tan and brown, with grayish-green moss growing on the shady walls like a moist embrace. Our progress took us toward the house where Marie would live in disgrace.

Mevrouw DeGroot's rooms in the Begijnhof were simple and clean. Inside there was a green mantle over a fireplace surrounded with blue Delft tiles. The floor was tiled in white and black, alternating like a chess board. A warm fire and wine were provided. I kissed Marie and felt relief that Mevrouw DeGroot was there, but I did not want to leave my sister. The rooms were clean and bright, however my sister was wounded in her heart. Who could know how to heal her? Could Mevrouw DeGroot? Should I stay here too? I could live with Marie and the nuns. I could do Marie's work. But how could I reach her pain? Her young face with sparse freckles stared into the black and white tiles as if the answer lay in the ground under her feet.

Mevrouw DeGroot said the nuns would be kind to Marie, and she would be allowed to stay if she worked in the garden and the kitchen.

I did not know how to explain to our Father what had happened or why Marie had left without saying goodbye, when he returned that day. I told him that Marie was sickened by a miasma from the canal, for there were many instances of foul odors wafting from the canals and sickening our residents. It felt less of a lie to say that the nuns had agreed to nurse her and that we would see her when she was well. I knew my lying would grow with Marie's belly.

Chapter Thirteen

Marie Changes

O ver the summer months I visited Marie as often as I could, but I was spending more time now with Father in the factory since his return. I took food to Marie and made her a wrap for the cold autumn to come. As Marie's belly grew, my body also made the mysterious changes accompanied with a girl becoming a woman. I hid the changes as best I could. I knew how these changes had condemned Marie.

When days were warm, Marie and I walked together under the willows, speaking quietly so as not to disturb the nuns and the quiet atmosphere. The grass muffled our steps as we walked to the edge of the canal to share our secret fears. The swans continued as peaceful sentinels. They appeared not to know the chaos in our minds.

Each time I saw her, Marie was bigger. Her work in the garden became more difficult. Her limbs and face looked thin, like a woman much older and wearier. When I walked home along the Minnewater I vowed that Father Bernardo would pay, but I had not seen him since that day at our home. I imagined choking him or stabbing him. In my mind I tossed his pierced body into the canal with the strength of one of our weavers, my hands bloody with retribution.

When Marie's time was due, Mevrouw DeGroot sent for me. I made an excuse to Father and walked to the Begijnhof. The quiet beauty of the cobbled streets belied the task I knew awaited me.

The air along the Minnewater blew cold and I pulled my woolen cloak close around my face. Tears and snot mingled under my nose as I walked. I knew not why I cried, but something was ending and I cried for that something.

In Marie's room it was warmer, and I swiped under my nose with my sleeve. The room contained a small cot, a chair and a crucifix. Marie was tossing from side to side on the straw-filled cloth. At times she suddenly pulled her legs up to her chest, making panting or grunting noises.

I knelt to hold her as she rocked and moaned. It reminded me of her earlier story of rocking and moaning. My beautiful Marie could do nothing to stop her pain, nor could I stop my own.

Mevrouw DeGroot wiped the sweat from her wet face and hair. I gave Marie chamomile tea. I felt helpless, afraid I might lose a beloved sister. I sang to her and rubbed her feet. Marie asked for very little, but she held my hand tightly when offered.

I knew nothing of babies or birth when I went to my sister that day. I had seen goose eggs hatch and had helped street dogs whelp in alleyways, but had not attended the birth of a child. Mevrouw DeGroot assured me that she and I could help Marie. No midwife was called, for Mevrouw DeGroot had borne seven children and knew what to do. I sent a note home to Father that Marie had taken a turn for the worse, saying that I would spend the night with her.

I stayed the night, holding Marie and fetching the items Mevrouw DeGroot needed for the birth. I brought water and rags. I held Marie's hand, patted her hair, washed her face, and tried to quiet her fears. When she wasn't sleeping between pains, I told her stories of the apprentices. She laughed weakly when I told her that Jan had brought flowers for me to take to her. I told her I thought he had stolen them from the garden next door. I pointed to them on the hearth. Their cheerful heads hung low from lack of water and being so near the fire.

I told her about lazy Basil "Meniere Cabbage Face" Cœcke who had taken to sleeping behind the great stack of spare heddles and thread, the smell of ale and cabbage stew sticking to his clothing. The others had pushed the large stack on top of him, but it failed to awaken him. Marie seemed too weak by then to laugh, but she squeezed my hand and smiled. The smile was that of a person setting out to travel to a distant shore alone.

I made up stories about the remaining tapestry workers.
I wanted to make Marie laugh again. There had been no
laughter between us for so long.

I told her stories of the other weavers. Adolph had
nearly cut off his little finger while sharpening scissors.
Dominicus had fallen in love with Désiré, his sister's best
friend, who Marie and I believed returned his affections.
Mauritius was soon to be let go by Papa if Papa did not
stop having to pull out all the poor weaving Mauritius had
done that day. Gustaf had been appointed to high office in
the weaver's guild—and on I went.

Jan, I reminded her, had no one with whom to play *Hot
Hands*. This was the game we three played where we would
guess whose hand was touching ours behind our back. I
remembered how Marie had squealed and flirted with Jan
during the game, and how Jan reddened when she touched
his hand. Sweet Jan—so desperately in love with my sister.

I invited her home to play to another game of *Queek*
with Geertruyd and me as soon as she was well. I told her
the checkered cloth was set out, ready for one of us to
call whether a thrown stone would land on a dark or light
color. I reminded her I had won the last time and that she
owed me one of her jars of cream for our chapped hands.

Marie worked very hard through the night to have the
baby. Sometimes she cried. Sometimes she slept. She did
not scream. I think she was too tired. By the time the babe
entered the world, Marie could barely hold her head off

the pillow. She smiled at the limp, blue form and whispered something I didn't hear. I baptized the still form, though I no longer believed in the dogma regarding the sins of the innocent.

There was so much blood after the tiny boy slid out from Marie. It poured from between her legs. We pressed clean cloths there and bound them in place, but soon enough of the blood seeped through and began leaking onto her thighs and the bed.

Mevrouw DeGroot did not seem to see the blood, but I was transfixed. It congealed on the rag as I tried to clean it off the floor. It sat in black shiny puddles, its smell leaving a metallic taste in my mouth. I nearly vomited, not from the sight of it, but because I knew I tasted my sister's death on my tongue.

As Marie appeared to sleep, gray in the face and covered with perspiration, I whispered more plans to her. I begged her not to leave me.

We would play again, I told her. This coming St. Nicholas Day, we would make the dried fruit-studded bread mother had made when she was still alive. On December 6th, we would leave our shoes outside again to receive the gifts St. Nicholas would bring. I petitioned her to please, please not leave me alone for St. Nicholas Day. I promised her my share of the walnuts from my shoes set out in the snow, if she would just live.

Throughout the night I watched her breathing. It was

quite rapid and shallow. I lay next to her on the bed, holding her in my arms, whispering to her that Father and I loved her always and for her to be strong for us. She said, "I'm cold. I'm so cold." I covered her with blankets, but she repeated her entreaty throughout the night.

In the morning, my sister was dead—my adored sister who had always been at my side, and who I believed would be my life-long companion. I had watched her life stream onto the floor in a black, slippery puddle.

My sister—who laughed, pulled at my bodice, threw chopped turnips down my chemise and told me stories in bed. My sister—whose beauty I would never match. My sister—whose youth and innocence were stolen by a man of God!

I rocked her cold body in my arms. I kept her covered with several blankets—for I thought, oddly—she should not be allowed to get so cold, though I knew she was dead. I rocked her until Mevrouw DeGroot said the men were here to take away the bodies of Marie and her dead baby, whom we had baptized as Jan, the same name as her sweet apprentice.

I walked along the canal in the chill that morning. I walked over the small bridges that led to our house with my eyes fixed ahead on the changing colors of the ivy curling up the stone houses, almost to their stepped roofs. I heard only my footsteps on the cobblestones. The people I passed were moving their lips, but I heard no sounds. I went home to explain everything to Father, for now Marie had nothing left to lose.

CHAPTER FOURTEEN

Claire's Plan

Back at the Art Theft Detail on Farralon Street, Artie stood in Simon's office to announce his intention of getting carryout for everyone before turning off the tape-recording of Paolo's confession and heading toward the door.

"I'll be back in about 30 minutes. I've got a large goat cheese and caramelized onion pizza waiting," he said as he picked up his keys and left Simon's office. Though I knew Artie was trying to make me feel better by getting my favorite pizza, I wished he wouldn't leave. I knew what was next.

Simon rose from his chair. We were alone together.

"I've notified the Vatican police," Simon said, "and when we're finished with the tape today I'll send it to them. They'll send someone in three days to retrieve Paolo and the tapestry."

"I don't know, Simon. He has a semi-believable story," I countered. "He's the love of Nora's life—or so she says—but I've heard that before. If he's telling the truth, he has to go up against the Vatican even though it's not a battle he's likely to win."

I waited. Past intimacy had never taught me to predict Simon's response. He could be sympathetic and gentle, or cold and brittle. That's the odd thing about old lovers. You're attracted to something that seems wonderful at the time, then that something turns on you. The flip side of that something becomes a thing you dread. His careful deliberation, which I thought was a rare commodity when we met, I now felt indicated a cold heart. He often dealt a hard hand.

"He won't win the battle without documents proving ownership," his voice was flat and free of compassion. He moved toward the door. He was finished. I wasn't.

It was hard not to look at the lean cut of his suit and his dark, coffee-colored hair. I remembered the feel of that hair while we made love. I remembered the smell of him—like dried wool and pencils.

The desire I felt still to my everlasting consternation, as well as his matter-of-fact pronouncement about the case, made my voice hard and edgy.

"Well, I'm interested in knowing if the Vatican has any."

"Any what?" Simon turned from the door looking at his desk, not at me. He seldom looked at my face. I knew the feeling. If I really looked at him I was lost.

"So far we don't know if the Vatican can prove ownership any more than Paolo can. We only know that they reported it stolen." I pulled eye drops from my pocket, threw my head back and put in the cool liquid. The stinging subsided temporarily and gave me time to collect myself. It was also a very handy way to mask tears, not that I had any in the pipeline.

"I understand they've had the tapestry for about 500 years, Claire. And, you're known to be a bit anti-Catholic since your years spent with the nuns, so you're not unbiased." This pronouncement came in an omniscient tone. I genuinely hated this about him. His pronouncements were made as if they were THE FACTS.

Nora had pointed out many times that in this regard I had chosen someone just like my Father: a man who had THE FACTS and who brooked no disagreement. I had told her she was crazy.

By now though, I knew she was right. What had I seen in him? Had he really been so condescending all this time? Did love and lust blind everyone equally or just those who were blind to begin with?

"Okay, okay, I admit I'm biased, but what if Paolo is telling the truth and the Vatican did steal it? It wouldn't be the first time the Vatican came by a work of art in a less than forthright manner. Look what happened during World War II. I want to take the tapestry to the Textile Museum in Laguna Beach and they'll look into its provenance."

I knew I was treading on thin ice. Simon was right to deny me this case. Nora's friendship with me created a conflict-of-interest so I should recuse myself from the case immediately.

He held himself very tightly. His arms were clutched to his chest. He seemed to pull himself inside to keep me at bay. My posture mirrored his.

I tried to look tall and intimidating. Suddenly I detested that smug, well-put-together face. I wanted to slap him just like I had wanted to, or maybe I did, the day he'd announced he was going back to his ex-wife: Meg. He was weak. What kind of idiot woman falls in love with a weak man? The conversation about going back to his ex-wife was fresh in my mind.

He'd said, "I-discovered-I'm-still-in-love-with-my-ex-wife." It came out just like that, all in one rush of a breath.

What? Simon and I had been lovers for a year. We had talked of marriage. Really, what was there to say? What was the appropriate answer? Where was my courage? Where was his?

I had begun to cry—the kind of desperate crying where inhaled hiccups come out but no words. It was embarrassing. It was humiliating. It was all I could do.

He had studied my red face. Had he been comparing me with Meg? He was a galling man. I'm not sure what I did or said that night. It wasn't pretty. I don't think I took it like a man or even like a lady.

Of course, that's why women's magazines don't recommend office relationships. Quadruple that recommendation for a relationship with your boss.

I kept my voice very calm and carefully modulated. My thoughts were on Paolo and Nora. "There's an expert on tapestries of this time period at the museum. I can't remember his name, but I met him once. I think he can help. Let me take it to him."

"Claire, this isn't your case anymore. The Vatican police will be here in three days to pick up the tapestry and take Paolo into custody." There was that final tone again.

I had enough. My hand came down on Simon's desk in a slap like an encyclopedia hitting a stone floor. "You can't let that happen!" I yelled so loud my voice had a guttural rasp. My damp hands inadvertently crumpled his papers. Some stuck to my palms but most went skidding to the floor.

I paced in front of him. My raspy voice turned barely audible. I spoke very slowly.

"You can't let that happen. You can give me three days, Simon. Three days. You can give me that."

He looked at me without speaking. I squared my shoulders, taking a deep breath. Looking out the window I said, "You owe me three days, Simon. You owe me that." Later on I realized how embittered I sounded. I went in for the kill.

"What you did to me was cowardly. I never said that to you because I was too shocked to think of what to say. I'm over it, as I can see you are too. I've lost a lover, Simon, but I won't lose a best friend."

"Claire," Simon answered quietly from his seat looking at his hands, "I can't do this. I know I 'owe' you. I know I made a hash of our life together."

"I, uh, I…" he got up from the chair, moved around the desk and took hold of me by the arms. He swallowed hard, meeting my eyes. I thought about spitting, but I didn't know how.

The air felt hot. I was too close to him. I didn't want him to touch me. I didn't want to cry.

"I know I've hurt you. I know that you can never understand why I went back to Meg. I do want to make it up to you. I should never have become involved with you in the first place. Claire, I'm so sorry."

His admission was unique. Usually he was Teflon-coated,

problem-free, and everyone else was at the core of any problem. He deflected responsibility like a shield on a sci-fi spaceship. Denial allowed him to sleep peacefully while a path of destruction led to his bed.

"Not half as sorry as I am, Simon." I shook off the grip of his arms and moved toward the door.

"I'm going to take the tapestry for three days. I'm going to take it and you're going to look the other way for three days," I stopped for another deep breath because I realized I had been holding my breath for so long my head hurt. I repeated in a low slow voice, "You're going to look the other way."

Simon stared, perspiration shining on his upper lip. He began to pick up the crumpled papers on the floor. He didn't look at me when he spoke.

"We didn't have this conversation," he said. "The tapestry is in the evidence room. It will be in the evidence room three days from now when the Vatican police arrive." He looked up. "It will be there, Claire. Promise me."

I met his gaze. After a long moment I summoned a quiet response, "I promise." But I couldn't leave it at that. I wasn't that noble. I opened the door and turned back to face him, "And that shows one of us can keep a promise."

Chapter Fifteen

Father Ardonne Visits

When I had explained everything to Father, his eyes were filled with tears and his mouth hung open like an old man's mouth, quivering and covered with snot. He put his head down on his desk and wept with long, shuddering sobs. I put my hand on his shoulder and left it there. He pulled the papers on the desk into a mass under his head, crumbling and weeping into them with abandon—rocking and weeping.

Later, I told him we must do something about Father Bernardo, but he did not seem to hear me. Perhaps he was unable to harbor revenge and grief in his heart at the same time, as I could and did. I not only harbored revenge, I stoked its fires as if a stag was to be thrown on to cook. Grief took its turn, but revenge was foremost in my thoughts, skating in circles like a man on an icy canal. Round and round my thoughts went, all ending with me savagely killing Father Bernardo. Indeed, he had now taken two souls to hell.

Work became Father's refuge again. We went about our business quietly, but we both worked without passion. We ate without appetite or interest. When evening came we often failed to light the candles, allowing ourselves to be engulfed by dark thoughts in dark rooms. Soup went cold, and clothes remained unmended. The fires guttered, but we were oblivious to the chill in the air. Conversations started and died on our tongues. Time moved—I knew because I saw the shadows against the roofs as they showered the canals with ghostly shapes, and those shapes moved into their winter hideaways.

And yet Father's tapisserie continued the garden verdure tapestry for Duke Campezzi, though a bit behind schedule because of Father's travels and our paralyzing grief. I said I would help with the work. The cartoon was finished and we were not allowed to make any changes to it by guild laws, but I had begun to think of a plan for the border. It was my way to avenge Marie's death.

I knew what I wanted in the border of the tapestry, but I did not tell Father. I wanted to tell the story of Marie. Nevertheless, I would have to tell it in symbols for her story was not a pretty one—not a story fit for a Duke's tapestry or a wedding.

I had seen the work of Rafæl on other cartoons and I knew how to amend drawings for the border, if I could steal the time. No one would notice or care. The weavers simply put the cartoon under their warp and worked away.

Father would not notice in his present state, nor did I intend to tell him, until it was too late to change.

I asked neighbors what had happened to Father Bernardo. I had not seen him since the day he was at our house. I heard that he had been promoted to the position of Monsignor and moved to Brussels. I asked Father if I could travel to Brussels, but he refused.

He shouted, "I will not lose another daughter! You cannot travel alone and I have no time to spare for you now, with the work you must do on the Duke's tapestry. You must forget about Father Bernardo, Beatrice." Father never shouted at me, but now everything in our world had changed. We did not speak of it again, neither the shouting nor our changed world.

As the months moved on and winter set in hard, I chose the symbols for the border and added them to the cartoons. Each symbol had a story of its own. I added a leopard, an orange tree, violets, and a crow. For Marie, I added strawberries, her favorite fruit. Revenge drove my cold fingers on the nights I stole my way into the tapisserie.

I was working late one dark afternoon after Father left to make purchases for the tapisserie. All the apprentices had gone home. I was alone in the shop when a knock came at the door. I pulled open the heavy door and saw a tall, slim man dressed in a black cassock. I did not recognize the man, but I knew the haughty stance of a priest. I felt the thrill of a chance to report Father Bernardo's attack.

"I am Father Philippe Ardonne," he said with a smooth voice and cold eyes. "I have come from the office of the Bishop. Are you Beatrice, daughter of Cornelius van Hecke?" I answered that I was and let him in, not knowing the reason for his visit.

I had been writing to the diocese for months since Marie revealed her pregnancy to me, letter after letter, yet I had not heard a word. Finally, a man had been sent to me to beg for forgiveness. He was tall, comely, and angular, but there was malevolence around his mouth. He stood in front of the fireplace and warmed his hands as he spoke.

"Well, Beatrice," he laughed softly, "you are much smaller than we had imagined, just a bit of a thing, in fact. In your letters to the Bishop you showed an independence that belies your age." He turned, gazing directly at my face. "How old are you?"

"Sixteen, Father." He moved to sit. He was graceful and handsome, but I shivered as if a flux was upon me. I remained standing.

"Then you can be forgiven for your naïveté. Your letters about Monsignor Bernardo have disturbed the Bishop, Beatrice. I am here to protect the interests of the Monsignor and the Bishop. Your accusations concerning the Monsignor show a misguided mind." He sat forward in the chair and raised a brow as he asked, very slowly, "Do you have a misguided mind, Beatrice?"

The smile lingered, like the diabolic figures in paintings

by Jheronimus van Aken, who signed himself Jheronimus Bosch.

"No, my mind is not misguided, Father Philippe," I insisted. "My sister is dead because of Monsignor Bernardo. I have written many letters to the Bishop and had almost given up. Will the Church do something to punish him?"

Could he hear my heart pounding? Did men of the Church have the power to look inside the soul and know our motives?

The fading smile renewed itself. "Oh, Beatrice, my child, your letters have only strengthened the Church's support of the Monsignor. We see daily that there are forces of evil ready to destroy the Roman Catholic Church."

My feeling of shock and disappointment must have registered on my face because it seemed to give him pleasure, and he continued. I looked around the warm, brown looms and behind the red, yellow and blue wools to see if any of the workers or Father might be near. I knew they had all gone. I knew my fate. I was alone with evil, as Marie had been. But I was not Marie, and I would kill this man if he made a move toward me—but with what weapon?

"Verily, Beatrice, we have a renewed resolve to do the work of Jesus Christ daily and to defeat the devil. I believe, Beatrice, sometimes the devil works through children like you or old men like your father. The devil takes the weak-minded and bends them to his will. When Satan does this, we find we must first offer the holy guidance of the

Church. If that is unsuccessful sometimes we must exorcise the devil by more, shall we say, *persuasive* means." At this he pulled his leather gloves until they were stretched taut.

"Persuasive?" I asked, my lips dry. I pulled my woolen wrap closer around my shoulders. I felt cold as he came out of the chair and moved closer to me to answer. I felt his breath on my cheek, just as Marie said she had felt the breath of Father Bernardo.

Father Ardonne spoke very quietly, "Sometimes, Beatrice, the Church must resort to fire and torture to make the devil leave the body. The devil can be quite relentless, but you have such a strong, young body." His eyes moved up and down over my body as he said it. "You could take the torture. Could your father take it, I wonder?"

I swallowed. My Father? He would hurt my Father?

He placed his gloves and hands inside his cassock and moved to the door. "Well, well, that may not be necessary. I'm sure your letter campaign is over. I have destroyed all of them. Will your father be home soon? Should I be asking him if the letters are finished?"

I shook my head, emitting a barely audible "No." My shawl had fallen from my shoulders, and the fire was low. I felt cold and damp in my armpits.

"I see that already the devil may be leaving hold of you, Beatrice. I see that our little talk has served your soul. It is so satisfying to do the work of the Lord our God," he said with a smile as he patted the leather gloves in his pocket.

He was gone and cold air rushed in as the door shut. I sat there until the fire died and it was time to cook supper for Father. I left the tapisserie to heat his soup. I did not tell him of the letters or the visit.

CHAPTER SIXTEEN

Claire Makes a Move

I retrieved the tapestry from the evidence room without incident. It was much easier than expected. I had concocted an elaborate lie about why I needed it, but found in the end that the evidence technician was too busy elsewhere to notice.

Alita Hanson, the technician, was authority-addicted—an evidence-room SS officer. Much of her time was spent assuring herself that her position in the cosmic order had not changed in the last ten minutes.

Alita's face had a severe beauty about it. Black hair was pulled tight into a vicious chignon. Her nose and cheeks were angular. Nothing about her felt curved, round, soft, warm or fuzzy. Her voice was like recycled aluminum cans in a trash compacter.

Alita was reaming another detective while I played nonchalant. She held her arms folded across her chest while she explained to him that without the appropriate paperwork the evidence was going nowhere. Sometimes I'm really quite proud of my ability to blend in with the woodwork. It's an act I've perfected over the years.

I look beige, I act beige. You would think I am innocuous. You would be wrong.

While Alita repeated the evidence room rules ad nauseum in a tone reserved for children under the age of six, I left the appropriate paperwork with Simon's forged signature. Alita was clearly not interested in my presence.

Getting the tapestry to the car was difficult. It was heavy, but I didn't want to involve Artie. It took a great deal of rolling to get it to my Mustang. The Vatican would have been appalled at my treatment of the tapestry. I was appalled. I was trained to revere and respect works of art. *Oh the hell with it.*

I headed south on PCH to the Textile Museum. I glanced in the rear-view mirror at the tapestry. I had this puppy for three days, and by god I would wrap up this mess by then.

Again I noticed the Persian carpet shops and espresso bars as I headed south through Corona del Mar to Laguna Beach. This time I was less terrified. Three days. *What was that, seventy-two hours? Piece of cake.*

The day was warm and the sky a crystal blue with no clouds. It's odd how that happens in Southern California— no clouds, not a whisp, not a cumulus or nimbus to be seen—just searingly blue sky.

Three days. I took a deep breath to empower myself. The sight of the jacaranda trees along PCH comforted me. They were an explosion of purple blossoms, like Chinese fireworks stopped mid-air. The joy of seeing the blossoms reminded me that I would have joy again after three days when I resolved this and was out to tea with Nora.

I reflected as I stopped at every red light, and there

must have been one every thirty feet on PCH, how Nora had been so much of my life. Nora even liked my mother, Valerie. I liked my mother too, even if she was passive and mindlessly chatty.

Once, when the three of us were out to dinner, mother was running on and on about costumes she was designing for a 1940s' adaptation of Shakespeare's *Much Ado About Nothing* at a playhouse in Costa Mesa.

"...So the shoulder pads are really giving me trouble, sweetheart," she said to me. "You know, these are the 1940s' shoulder pads. They're not the bionic shoulder pads of *Dallas*. I'm really going for authenticity here. The look should be lean and elegant."

"Uh huh, Mom." I had felt the consciousness being sucked out of my brain by the costume design patter. I loved my mother but knew not one iota about plays, costumes, or the 1940s.

Mother looked to Nora instead. "Nora, you know what I mean when you have a look you're going for. It's like putting a Chinoiserie chair in a rustic cabin. You know what I mean, don't you dearie," Valerie had patted Nora's hand while I rolled my eyes behind Mom's back.

"Oh, Mrs. D, don't I know it, it would be all wrong," Nora made a face. While the two went on about anachronistic design faux pas throughout the luncheon, I did a mental grocery list. This was how it worked. Nora blathered on. I listened, or pretended to.

Later Nora had said, "I just love Valerie. She's such a hoot. I know you two have 'issues' but she's so not you. How did you two come to be related? She's so unconcerned about what others think of her. I like that about her. How'd she ever come to marry your dad? He's so, uh, emotionally constipated."

"I haven't the vaguest idea," I had replied. "What she sees in him is a mystery to us all." It was a mystery—one I had thought of often. What did she see in him? What did I see in Simon, once upon a time? Would I end up with someone as critical as my father? I had rather eat dirt every day for the rest of my life.

Dad was always there to tell you what to do and what you did wrong, I had told Nora. "Whatever my sister, Annette, and I did, it was the wrong thing."

"Yeah, he is a bit puffed up, and listening to him you would think he was the chief of military operations in the Pacific instead of a lit professor at U.C. Irvine, but he has some charms." Nora seemed to be trying to dredge up something nice to say no matter my objections.

"You know, sometimes I think Annette and I could be perfectly normal human beings right now if we'd had normal parents," I mused.

She smiled sympathetically and leaned a warm hand on my arm. "Well, what is normal?" was Nora's reply. "My mom didn't know my dad was gay until they were married for thirty years. You think that's normal? The worst is over. It's in the past."

Was it in the past?

Dad could still take pleasure in reducing Annette and me to tears. Mother would say, "Now Jim," but she never ventured beyond that.

When we were young, he resorted to slaps when the mood

suited him and he was not satisfied with verbal abuse. By the time we were adults, Annette and I had moved out and our contact with him was limited. We forgave Valerie for her lack of courage. But had we forgiven ourselves for ours?

Looking back over my life at home, dad was a vortex of whirling resentment into which my little life's ship had stalled. Like an emotional maelstrom, waves of sarcasm rolled into and away from him, engulfing and drowning all those in his path. I often wondered if he suffocated his students as well, or did they sail sturdier ships? Surely they know how to steer clear of the maelstrom via a longer, but calmer sea route.

Nora had deflected all of that by waving off old, long-buried esteem issues and bolstering me when my love life waxed and waned—more waning than waxing. She was the sister/mother who could be there for me because she wasn't involved in fending off her own emotional terrorism.

A four-year live-in arrangement with Andy Keen, my linguistics professor, had ended just as I met Nora. Nora called him "Andy the Eye Candy" and told me that he really wasn't my kindred spirit. Andy was too interested in himself. I knew this all along but pretended not to notice. However, I did learn a valuable lesson about eye candy and promised myself I wouldn't repeat the lesson.

Nora liked to remind me that all of it was *a process*. This was her favorite reaction to life events. Ending a relationship? *It's a process.* Facing a life-changing event? *It's a process.* Losing your mind? *It's a process.* Expansion and contraction of the universe? *It's a process.*

I was stopping at the twenty-ninth red light to allow

pedestrians with surf boards to cross the street. What was the point of this? Both sides of the street were the same anyway. Of course there was that ocean on the right side that people always wanted to see.

I waited while three teenage boys with spiked hair, no shirts, and mid-calf shorts ran across PCH with bare feet.

For several years Nora tried to fix me up with her clients, old friends, school chums and fitness coaches. My heart wasn't in it. When I met Simon, Nora gave me the kind of solid direction a best friend would give.

"Jesus, Claire, he's your boss! Are you nuts? Why can't you just date Winston Cole? What was wrong with him?" Winston was a devastatingly handsome black gentleman who was a fellow designer.

"Because I can't stand Winston Cole, Nora. He makes a clicking sound with his teeth." Nora had given up, and my relationship with Simon took off only to crash a year later with the ex-wife fiasco. However, Nora was too good of a friend to rub my nose in it.

"Claire, Simon just couldn't let you be you. It's that simple. He's not a bad man, he's just unsatisfied with the status quo. He wants to make you different so he'll feel better about himself," Nora summarized. God she was brilliant. She should have her own daytime television program.

I knew she was right, but I needed to mourn. So mourn I did, protractedly. I looked at the three boys almost at the other side of PCH heading for the ocean to catch a wave and celebrate the day. It was time to live in the present—the boys were a sign from the universe.

I glanced again at the business calendar on the front seat.

Why couldn't I remember the textile expert's name? I saw it again on today's date: Davies, Mark Davies. I had met him somewhere but couldn't recall where. He must have been quite unremarkable.

I turned to some classical guitar on the radio. It sounded like Christopher Parkening, one of my favorites. I was thinking of Bach and Parkening when I remembered where I had met Davies. I was with Simon working a case and had met him in a round of introductions at the museum. For the life of me I couldn't conjure up a face.

Belatedly I realized I had missed the museum driveway on PCH. I would have to drive beyond Main Beach and try to make a left turn. *What an idiot!* I would be late for the appointment.

Tourists were everywhere walking and talking with caramel apples in their hands, paying no heed to the left-turning traffic. Main Beach is the most crowded pedestrian venue in Laguna Beach, where muscled beach boys play volleyball to impress fawning under-dressed girls—summer or winter.

Providence allowed me a quick turn into Forest Avenue at Main Beach to circle back onto the Coast Highway. I was back at the museum parking lot behind the Mexican restaurant on Aster. I almost ignored the view, which was breathtaking. There was the Pacific Ocean, right next to me.

The cool air-conditioning met my face as I entered the low, dark, marbled entryway. The air smelled of old fabrics, and I stepped in to get a better look at the Laguna Beach Textile Museum. It was a two-story structure with quiet, wooden floors and subdued colors on the wall so as not to compete with the textiles on display. Today there was an exhibition of nineteenth century American quilts and seventeenth century Flemish lace. I wandered briefly through the entry to the exhibits.

I had a vague recollection of meeting the museum staff with Simon. A tall, slim woman of indeterminate age approached me as a member of the staff and asked, "May I help you?"

"Yes, I have an appointment with Dr. Mark Davies. My name is Claire DeMaer." I pronounced it <u>DeMayor</u> carefully for the woman, because the name tended to throw people. Flemish names have vowels thrown in for no apparent reason.

"Oh yes, he mentioned your appointment, I'm his assistant, Susan Price. Let me take you to his office," the slim woman answered. She led the way at a brisk, efficient pace. I wished I could look so put together. How did she manage to make no sound and glide on the wooden floor with those high heels? Heels were a mystery to me and tended to make me walk like a geisha.

After a brief elevator ride and walk through a darkened hall, I was led to Davies's office. Susan Price made introductions, getting my name right, and ducked out.

I extended my hand to Davies, but he managed to speak first while shaking my hand.

"Detective DeMaer, it's a pleasure. I'm Dr. Mark Davies, but please call me Mark. From your phone call I ascertain that you and I are about to spend three full days together."

He moved quickly from the handshake to gesture toward two chairs flanking a massive cherry desk. The office was one of cordial disarray. Exhibition posters were propped up against the wall and large books were opened on an expansive table next to the desk. The books were in haphazard stacks with sticky notes extending from their edges like sailing flags announcing conditions in a paper sea.

"Lucky for you, we have just launched the exhibits you saw when you came in, so our push is over and I can set aside some of the more mundane work. I also just finished writing a grant, so I needed a break. Please have a seat." He indicated a metal chair.

His handshake was warm, firm and confident. I thought I could feel at home in an office like this. The place had a different feel than the gray cubicle on Farralon Street. It was messy in an organized way and I pictured Dr. Davies as a modern Mr. Chips, with elbow patches and too many papers to grade.

"Dr. Davies—Mark," I said, rearranging myself in the chair, "I appreciate you taking my call and working me into your schedule. I have the tapestry with me in the car and would appreciate some help getting it inside."

Mark pushed a button on his phone for assistance. Car keys were handed over to a young man who appeared in the doorway to retrieve them and make the trip to the car.

We chatted about friendly, social nonsense until the tapestry was brought into the room. "Set it here, Roy," Mark said to the young man as he pushed books to the side and covered a large table near his desk quickly with a clean, white cloth. The tapestry was set on the cloth carefully. I could see they treated art treasures with respect here at the museum, unlike the way I rolled the tapestry through the parking lot back on Farralon.

Roy left, and Mark washed his hands before looking at the tapestry. He donned a pair of white cotton gloves as he said, "Well, since we have no time to waste let's just open this up."

I studied the top of his head as he gingerly unwrapped the tapestry. It was a nice head, as heads go. No laughable ears, no ridiculous long hairs stretched sideways over a bald patch, no earrings or facial piercings that I could see. No back-of-the-neck tattoos, thank God. His spiky, brown hair with fringes of gray rested quite nicely on his head, and the immediate impression was one of a hip scholar. *Was that an oxymoron?*

He'd taken off his suede jacket while we had waited for the tapestry, and I noticed now that he was wearing faded jeans and a black T-shirt.

I had the impression that under that T-shirt was a strong chest. Not the over-developed pectorals of the exercise obsessed, but just a firm body. Nice head, nice body, nice hands.

"Detective, may I call you Claire?" he asked.

"Of course, I'm sorry, I should have said that immediately since we are going to be working together so closely for the next few days." *Good Lord was I staring at the man's pecs?*

"So Claire, tell me this story again. I believe you said on the telephone that in three days the Vatican police will be taking the gentleman you mentioned into custody and, with him, the tapestry. So what is it you hope we can unearth about this tapestry in three days?" he asked.

He spoke with an open expression and ended with a wide smile. He had great teeth, white and straight. Parents must have footed a bill for braces long ago. I didn't have an older brother, but it seemed like Mark had an older brother face. It was calm and trustworthy. He also had an expression that proclaimed he knew an inner joke you didn't know.

I related Paolo's story with all the salient details while Mark slowly perused the tapestry. When I finished I stopped and waited for his response. He looked up.

"So Detective Claire, if I'm reading between the lines, you're really not supposed to have this tapestry because the Vatican is now in charge of this investigation. But the life of a textile museum curator is lacking a bit in the hanky panky department, so I won't put you on the spot about why you have this tapestry. I'll savor the moment. Just let me know how many laws I'm breaking as we speak."

I felt flames above my collar, and after a moment's hesitation decided to give Mark the benefit of the doubt. I relayed the entire story, including losing Nora's friendship and defying my boss. I left out the ex-lover part.

As I described it, the situation sounded like reality television. Sordid. I couldn't imagine why my lips were still moving. *Had I had a stroke and couldn't stop talking?*

The man would be rolling up the tapestry any minute, asking me to leave. Or guffawing. Or calling Simon.

"Well, well, that beats writing up three-fold programs explaining early Plains quilt patterns any day. In fact, it allows me to get closer to my true passion, which is tapestry of the period you have here in front of you. I've written several articles on the topic and am working on a book about tapestry right now, so your tapestry is a welcome intrusion. And I don't mind the faint hint of the forbidden."

The Bruges Tapestry

That smile, with a slight dimple on one side, again crept across his face. I felt relief and, for the first time since arresting Paolo, a stirring of hope.

I asked, "What can we get done in three days? What are you able to tell from this in such a short amount of time? How can we get at the true owner by just looking at the tapestry?"

He held up both gloved hands. "Whoa! I'm not a miracle worker!" he laughed. "I don't know that you and I can accomplish anything." At that I suddenly felt dejected and my shoulders drooped.

He saw me deflate and said, "Right now we're just going to take a look at what you have here. We'll look at the central field, the borders, the pattern of the weave, the subject matter in the weaving, any lettering on the front or back of the tapestry, and the colors used. We'll also look for a weaver's mark, although it's probably too early to have one, and from there we'll see what we find. We'll inspect these things for so long you'll wish you'd taken up another line of work. Then we'll order dinner."

"Do you like Italian?" he said, without a hint of irony.

Chapter Seventeen

A Special Meeting

After the visit from Father Ardonne, I decided to be more cautious in my dealings with the Church. I couldn't continue to write letters. The Bishop had not responded, and my fears for Father were pressing on my heart. If they hurt him, I had no one in the world. Marie was gone. Father's safety was on my mind at all times.

I worked at the factory as I had before, but now I worked furiously on the border. A colleague of Ambrosius Benson had designed the central field and border. I continued to make careful amendments to it alone after everyone had left the tapisserie.

I had to make the story of Marie come alive in the border, but it could not be so obvious as to awaken the attention of the Duke, whom I had not yet met. There was no reason to believe the Duke would allow me to take such liberties with the border, but he need not know.

If I could weave the story of Marie and the treachery of

the Church into the tapestry, it would be there for all to see— hidden in plain view. The Duke would never know, but the message would be there, ready for me to reveal the true nature of the Church when it was safe to do so. For now I was safe and so was Father.

As the time for the completion of the tapestry approached, Father became more distracted and spent long hours at work. He feared we would not finish in time, incurring the wrath of the Duke. I wondered if the Duke was as formidable as he seemed based on my Father's admonitions to me and to the weavers.

Father announced that the Duke would be arriving shortly to see the work in progress. This was highly unusual. The Duke was on his way to Mechelen to negotiate with the bride's family and wished to see his wedding gift, yet unfinished.

Everyone felt the excitement of the Duke's arrival. Father paced, and the apprentices shouted and waved their hands. Tapestry weaving is a slow process and no amount of shouting or hurrying allows it to proceed with greater haste. The Duke would have to be prepared to see his tapestry well before it was completed.

I had always loved the pace of the weavers with their work-hardened hands moving weft through the warp at a slow, easy pace. It took months or years for the image of the cartoon to be woven onto the surface of the warp.

Each weaver had a special ease with a specific kind of

image. Adolph showed a keen interest in animal images, while Dominicus had a hand for the floral designs. Mauritius did all the finishing work. Achiel and Francois could render sky and architecture when called for, and our sweet Jan was a particular genius for weaving hands and faces. Willem could make fabric folds appear to shimmer on the surface and could weave brick or stonework to make one think a stonemason had taken up weaving. Each work called for special gifts, and this mille-fleur for the Duke kept Dominicus very busy.

On the day the Duke was to arrive I smoothed my hair in place under a green velvet hood that came to point under my chin, covering a white linen coif. I had taken pains to dress in my finest yellow silk skirt. I had sewn the skirt from yellow silk in my mother's wardrobe. I thought the yellow set off something in my eyes, though I had no intention of looking the Duke in the eyes—such a thing would be unseemly.

I wore matching green and yellow brocade sleeves. The Duke would take no notice of me, of course, but I wanted Father to be proud of his daughter and of his work.

The townspeople knew of the Duke's visit, and word had spread that his entourage was already making its way past the Market down Sint Amandstraat. My dearest friend, Geertruyd, ran all the way to our workroom to tell me she had seen the Duke himself!

"Oh he is of fine countenance, Beatrice!" Geertruyd said

while catching her breath. She put her hands aside her head as she said, "His cap is made of dark blue velvet and rests on his head like so, with gold braiding running across the three points," with this she demonstrated a cap with points over the ears and a central point in the front. Her cheeks were flushed red with the excitement of the Duke's arrival.

"He is tall and stately on his horse, and his robe is the color of the sky in the evening. Beatrice, even his horse is wearing velvet! His hair, well, I can't remember the color, but it protrudes from under his cap, so he is not bald." This made me laugh as Geertruyd had an unusual dislike for baldness. She had wild, curly red hair stuffed under a linen cap that always snuck out in tendrils so that she swiped them viciously into position, especially when nervous.

Once Geertruyd had pointed to the cheesemaker's son, a young man she admired, and pronounced that she could marry such a young man because he had a splendid head of hair under his white cap. She believed the magnificent mane would make up for the smell of curds, which would surely invade her home and cling to her clothing if he was her husband.

Geertruyd continued her description with her hands waving in the air as I hurriedly cleaned the workroom and asked Mauritius to prepare warm wine. Geertruyd leapt behind me as the Duke's attendant pushed open our door and announced, "His Excellency, Duke Giulio Campezzi enters here!"

I curtsied immediately, with my head down. I could see only the fine, soft leather of his shoes and dark blue hose bearing tassels at the sides. Father bowed. I felt Geertruyd standing on to the back of my skirt. She cowered behind me with her head bowed low.

"Please do rise. I bid you speak to me concerning the progress of this arras," said the Duke, coming straight to the point and gesturing forward as if he knew the way.

I rose and took a deep breath. Geertruyd was right. He was comely, but much younger than I expected. He looked to be only slightly older than myself. I had expected an old man with bulging veins and sagging stockings. He looked kind, but imperial, and I knew to keep my own council. He did not speak to me but strode to the loom while speaking to Father.

Yes, he really was quite handsome. Geertruyd whispered loudly in my ear that he smelled of lavender and mint. No doubt he bathed more often than Meniere Cabbage Face. An Italian aristocrat might bathe even so much as once a month, I surmised, and might smell of herbs rather than cabbage. I knew lavender and mint to be the proper herbs for keeping fleas from the clothing, and I reckoned that he must have a fine attendant to prepare and keep his woolens. His mantle was particularly fine, with gold and silver embroidery around the neckline.

I envisioned his home in Italy, though I had no knowledge of Italy or even of an aristocratic home. Herbs and flowers such as daisies, fennel, roses, basil and violets would be sprinkled on the floor to keep his rooms sweet-smelling, and his bedstraw would be mixed with lavender and tansy to keep the bugs away. I imagined my worn, leather shoes crushing violets and scenting my skirt hem.

I could hear him saying "...very pleased to learn that the weaving is almost finished, Meniere van Hecke. My betrothed and I will journey to Bruges upon my return, and at that time I will be expecting to pick up the completed work. I trust it will be finished by then. We cannot be delayed in our travels to the Vatican for the wedding."

He had a deep voice with silken tones. His Italian was musical, and his lips moved more decidedly than ours did. It seemed rather funny to me that his mouth pouted forward, and I stifled a laugh by biting my cheeks.

"No, no of course not, Your Excellency. The tapestry will be completed. As you can see, it is nearly complete now. He gestured to me and told me to come over, "My daughter, Beatrice, and I will oversee the completion of the tapestry. Place yourself at ease."

Father was talking very fast. He was speaking Italian, but I was able to follow most of it. I attempted a response in Italian from where I stood because Geertruyd still stood on my skirt, but the Duke held up his hand.

"I speak Flemish, Mejuffrouw van Hecke," he said. His lips moved carefully around the Flemish syllables and, rather than being funny, I felt him attempting my language was a kindness he did for me.

We switched to Flemish and although I said little, I watched the Duke as my Father explained how we worked. The Duke seemed very interested. I had not expected such a man. Could I say he was a man? He could be no more than twenty years old. He was an interesting mix with the low voice and somewhat aged eyes of an older man, but the calves and waist of a young man.

"So I will be staying here for a few weeks to prepare for my journey to Mechelen, or do you call it Malines? Though Emperor Charles is in Spain, his aunt is in Mechelen—a place that seems quite distant right now. I will return from time to time during the next few weeks to see the progress on the tapestry. Mejuffrouw van Hecke, you will be here to explain the work, yes?" He turned to me and I saw now that those old man eyes were brown, the light brown of caramelized onions in marmalade with raisins, my favorite dish, sweet and savory.

I nodded yes, bowing slightly and holding myself stiff as a tree, swallowing a lump like three-day old bread. "Yes, of course, Your Excellency. I will be at your disposal." I attempted a deeper bow with Geertruyd still impaling my skirt.

After he left, Geertruyd and I stared for a long time at the hind end of his horse, holding each other by the hand. "Oh he has a fine leg, Beatrice! Did you see his shapely calves?" she asked as she turned to me. "What if he has to marry an ugly Austrian woman with hair on her chin, Beatrice?" Geertruyd was quite imaginative.

"Oh Geertruyd, such drivel you speak! She must be a beautiful young lady who plays the lute, has rivers of lace on her gowns and has hair filled with pearls that are as white as the Bruges swans. He will fall in love with her the minute he sees her and she will have a great dowry filling many trunks. She will have land and jewels, and they will travel together to be married by the Pope. Such a marriage will be blessed with many children." This sounded too fantastical even to my ears.

"Well, we shall see when he brings her back. I still think she will be ugly with a dowry full of chin hairs," Geertruyd nodded.

I continued to stare at the retreating entourage of the Duke. I wished for his Austrian fiancé to be struck suddenly hirsuit, as I felt my own chin distractedly.

To my surprise, the Duke came into the tapisserie the very next day and many days thereafter. He did not seem in such a hurry to travel to Mechelen. He asked a great many questions about the weaving process, just as Marie and I had asked when we were children. He seemed genuinely delighted with my answers, and his caramel eyes danced.

We walked together through the tapisserie as I explained the way the cartoon was placed behind the warp threads in order to weave the picture from behind, and he peering behind the warp as the weaver worked. He watched as Jan cut the threads in the back of the tapestry and guided new thread between the warp threads as the design changed.

"There is a great deal to learn here, Beatrice, you seem to have an affinity for your work," he commented as he took long strides. He held his hands clasped behind his back and I thought it might be fun to play *Hot Hands* with him, touching his hands to see if he could guess who had touched him.

I blushed at his use of my given name. Surely, this was unintentional.

His legs were long and well-formed as Geertruyd had said, in dark purple stockings. Today he wore a beautiful linen shirt under a short robe of purple and gold brocade. The sleeves were split open along the long outer seam and lined with purple velvet.

I wondered what a man in finery thought about, what he worried over. Surely his needs were always attended to by faithful servants, ready at his elbow. Was he thinking of his lady or his wedding?

"Oh yes, Your Excellency," I replied and hurried to keep up with his stride while keeping my eyes low. "I have been very happy here. I love this tapisserie. You will be astonished when you see the final tapestry. My Father's work is widely admired, as you must have already known to send a commission to him. He is as well-regarded amongst the guild members as he is through Flanders."

We walked through the factory to continue outside. The day was warm and the leaves swayed gently. The air smelled of wild flowers and sage.

A small, brown bird perched at the edge of an upended soup pot resting near the back gate. I must have left the pot there after throwing vegetable leavings into a heap near the garden soil. I could see now how shabby our small tapisserie and home must look to him. Brown flower heads, brown birds, a soup pot—it must all seem commonplace and vulgar to such a man. My eyes settled on my skirt and I swept dirt from the front of it. Surely he was accustomed to more exotic flora and fauna, as well as to more exotic company.

I had not felt my position so acutely before. I was an artisan's daughter and felt respected among my father's peers. I would someday be wedded to an artisan's son, perhaps one from the painter's guild, for we often worked with them in purchasing cartoons. It seemed a good life, though an unpretentious one.

I was uncomfortable walking at his side, maneuvering to stay behind him slightly to show respect while trying to keep my head lowered as I described the workings of the weavers.

"Tell me, Beatrice, why do you not stay home with your mother and learn the duties of a wife? Or do I tread in conversation where a man does not belong? In Italy you would be married by now."

The question came naturally and he appeared undisturbed by it, yet I turned my head to hide the heat in my face. The question of my marriage was seldom raised, and memories of my mother and sister still brought hot tears I could not allow him to see. I would act as my Father's ambassador—a composed lady.

Head low and eyes down, I answered carefully, "My mother died a short time ago. Since that time my sister and I have helped Father in the factory. Had helped, I should say. My sister also died."

I said this without weeping. Perhaps my heart was becoming a stone, a hard-edged stone, which I could use to hone hatred and revenge against Monsignor Bernardo. How could such a man have been elevated to monsignor!

"I am sorry to speak of this painful subject. You are very young for so much tragedy," the Duke said softly and made a slight bow, as if to atone for his faux pas.

He looked in my eyes briefly as I glanced up, and I felt the company of a sad soul. Perhaps there was more to the Duke than Geertruyd and I could imagine. Perhaps he was more than comely calves and a mantle that smelled of mint. Nevertheless, I could never know because a Duke and a weaver's daughter are from two different worlds that do not meet, except to discuss the delivery of goods by a servant to a lord.

"Yes, Your Excellency, very young for so much tragedy."

I bowed lower, feigning the need to check on a task in the factory, and begging permission to leave the Duke in the garden.

The Duke continued his visits despite my growing concern that it was awkward to remain in his company unattended. I looked forward to his questions during our walks in the garden, and when he was not there I busied myself with weaving the border. Father was busy with other commissions.

As time progressed, I began to write to Pope Leo X— Father Ardonne be damned—but no reply came. I supposed that Monsignor Bernardo flourished, while my sister's skin and bones withered in the ground. Tears came to my eyes as I remembered the wink Marie had given me before she closed herself in Father's study with Monsignor Bernardo. She had leaned out the door, winked, and placed her finger on her nose to remind me of my remark about him smelling like cat piss.

I wrote more letters and each was more vitriolic than the one before. To diminish my rage, I worked furiously on the border. One day as I was alone in the tapisserie drawing a crow into the cartoon border for another worker to weave, I felt suddenly overwhelmed by loneliness. I put my head on my arms and leaned onto the hard wooden table. I gave myself over to tears not shed for some time. Laughter had disappeared from my life. Father worked late each day, his eyes growing heavy under dark lids. There was as little affection in his conversation as there was conversation to be had with him.

I heard footsteps and lifted my head. The Duke stood before me. He reached into a leather pouch at his waist, pulling out a heavily embroidered linen cloth for my nose. He held the linen to my nose and made a gesture for me to blow. In my grief I scarcely noticed the humiliation of it. In fact, I was making hiccupping sounds while I wiped at my face with his elegant handkerchief.

"I'm so sorry, Your Excellency," I began, but the weeping overtook me again, and I put my hands over my face. I wept hard and long, not caring if His Excellency had me flogged.

Finally, he gently pulled my hands away. "No, no Beatrice, you must not apologize. I apologize for interrupting your sorrows. Is there something I can do? Could I bring a confessor to hear your troubles?" he asked as he leaned over me, his hand resting atop mine.

"No! No!" I shouted and he looked startled. "I mean, thank you, no. That will not be necessary, Your Excellency." I made desperate attempts to wipe my nose and recover some dignity. It would do no good to ruin my Father's reputation and character through ill-advised behavior.

"Perhaps you would be willing to tell me of your distress," he offered. He sat nearby at the wooden table, his brocade and velvet garments settling against the faded wood.

Certainly he must have much more important tasks I thought, but kept this to myself. I had no one to speak with about my family, and I longed to unburden this sorrow.

The Duke was without an entourage today. I did not recall seeing them during his last visit either. I hardly cared. I missed my sister more than words could express. My mind wandered to her constantly. I missed her humor and warmth and mischief.

"Your Excellency, you are too kind. It is a shocking story, perhaps your lordship would not think so highly of my family if it is told," I ventured, my head held low. Surely we were mere merchants to him—not of his world—beneath him in birth, behavior and social status.

He actually laughed. "Beatrice, in Italy we invented the shocking story! Why don't you tell me, and I will let you know if I am shocked." His hands rested now in his lap, but his stockinged leg was close enough to mine that I could feel the heat of his thigh. I moved away slightly. The heat of him was disquieting.

We sat near the quiet loom together. I began the story. The light slowly left the windows as the afternoon progressed. I was too weary to light the candles and too aggrieved to notice how close he sat.

I left out nothing, except how the tapestry border held the symbols of Marie's story. I ended with my interest in revenge, letters to the Bishop, and now to Rome where the Holy Father resided. Then I realized that the Holy Father was the one who would marry the Duke to his betrothed, and I felt confused and miserable.

He turned his soft eyes onto my wretched face. "This is a shocking story, Beatrice, but not for the reasons you think. I am shocked that your sister met with such misery, but more than that, I am appalled that members of the clergy act in Bruges as they do in Florence. Where is this coward, Father—no, Monsignor Bernardo? Let me speak with him." He looked gallant in the failing light, but I knew he was no match for Rome. Even an aristocrat from Italy was bound by the codes of the Roman Catholic Church: a force more powerful than kings and princes.

"I have not seen him for many months. I believe he is in Brussels. There is nothing to be done now. You must go on to Mechelen, meet your fiancé and marry in Rome." Too bad I could not send him on an errand to speak to his Holiness for me. What a thought. I must truly be mad.

Where I had barely thought of the Duke's marriage before, now it felt like another stinging loss. But why? I could not lose what I did not have. The Duke was not mine, not now or ever. Revealing my soul did not mean that we were, or ever could be, equals. A simple conversation did not elevate my status to that of Cecilia Haghenbeek— the name of his betrothed. Geertruyd had found it out somehow, gossiping with the Duke's horseman. She was a cousin of Margaret of Austria—the Aunt of Emperor Charles V. I supposed that their marriage had been planned since their births, probably for land holdings, though it was not my business to know or ask about it.

"Beatrice, since we are telling shocking tales, I will tell you mine." He hesitated and walked toward the dying light at the window. His handsome figure, covered in velvet, cast a dark silhouette. He faced the window as he spoke. His low voice sounded older and weaker than moments earlier.

"I have no desire to go to Mechelen," he spoke as if to a confidante.

"I have not had the pleasure of meeting Lady Haghenbeek. She has been betrothed to me since birth. This is my duty to my family. Such an alliance is important to my father's business in the wine trade, and to her family in the shipping trade. So you and I both have our sorrows, and we both contend with our family obligations. Without the wine trade and my betrothed, I would be inclined to stay in Bruges for some time, but my parents would be displeased—very displeased."

"It seems," he finished, "our lives are not our own. We are both bound by family matters."

I was listening intently. Only now did I notice that the Duke had returned from the window, and for the last remark his hand had rested over mine. Now he wound his fingers around mine and brought them near his lips. I was both comforted and disconcerted. There could be nothing to come of a craftsman's daughter and a Duke. My mouth felt dry; my breath caught in my chest.

"You would stay in Bruges, Your Grace?" My voice cracked like crumpled parchment.

With his eyes tightly closed, he kissed my fingertips. "I would, Beatrice, stay in Bruges—to help you and to avenge your sister's death." He whispered and leaned toward my mouth. I was holding my breath.

Then came a sound from the doorway. The Duke broke off from me immediately, giving the slightest bow, and speaking loudly enough for any interlopers nearby, "Mejuffrouw van Hecke, I thank you for the demonstration of weaving." He left through the garden door at the side of the tapisserie.

Father Ardonne opened the door.

"Good evening again, Mejuffrouw," he said, pulling his leather gloves slowly off his hands.

"Well, well, Beatrice. I see that you have inherited your sister's charms. Monsignor Bernardo told me she was a seductress, what was her name again? Marguerite? No, Marie—I believe that was it. Now you use your feminine wiles on the Duke. It really will not help you, you know. Your letters have gone too far, and no one can help you now," Father Philippe moved forward, towering over me.

My legs felt as if they were nailed to the wooden bench.

My heart was pounding at the mention of Marie's name.

"What do you mean, 'no one can help me now'?" I asked, backing up as he advanced until stopped by the loom. There was a sickly sensation of vomitus in my throat, which I swallowed heavily.

"The Monsignor is very powerful. He has the backing of Rome now owing to my influence and his wealth. Did you know that he was a very wealthy man? I am confident that he will be elevated to Cardinal very soon, and then our little plot will run smoothly," he continued as he walked back and forth.

What plot? To kill my family?

"And to be dogged by the likes of you, a doxy, congeals my blood. A harlot is nothing, a vessel only to be used as men command. No one would miss you. I doubt your father would even notice you were gone." He reached for a wisp of hair that had escaped my coif and touched it lightly. I slapped at his hand.

"Be careful, Beatrice," he said rubbing at his hand. "The canals are dangerous, and one can come to harm just walking near them. Do you swim, Beatrice?" He smiled as one with a sword would while fighting a man armed with a feather.

I shook my head. My throat felt very tight and dry. It was difficult to breathe, the air insufficient and malignant.

He leaned toward my skirt and lifted a heavy bunch of fabric into his hand. "No? Pity—I believe those thick skirts would take you down quite rapidly. It would be dark and cold. No one would hear you cry out. It would be such a pity—so many losses for your father to endure, yes?" Again, the vicious smile arose.

He was so close now I could smell the spirits on his breath. I wanted to strike his face hard.

He pulled away abruptly and called out to the other room, "Enough Mejuffrouw. I have other church matters to attend to and must take my leave." He turned to look back adding, "You will take care when walking near the canals, yes?"

CHAPTER EIGHTEEN

Claire and a Reluctant Invitation

W e still hadn't stopped for dinner, despite the earlier offer of Italian from Mark. He was bent over the tapestry in the waning evening light. He'd appeared intrigued since the moment he had unrolled it.

He said the workmanship was exquisite. It was most certainly Flemish as he had proposed, probably from the early sixteenth century. He muttered facts about the tapestry as he examined it. I listened for something I could use but only heard academic mumbling.

I busied myself with looking around his space to learn more about this man. He looked preoccupied with the tapestry. I glanced at books on the shelf that were mostly about Christian symbols in art or tapestry this and that. On his desk was a newsletter from the Society of Creative Anachronism, whatever that was. He had a sort of tidy disarray going on in the office. I noticed several books authored by him as I perused the shelves. Tapestry and textiles were his thing. It seemed rather odd for a man.

He must be a fascinating partner at a dining table. He was cute though. I liked his firm biceps and buzzed, slightly graying hair. Then I realized he had just said something about the sixteenth century while I had been shamelessly inattentive.

"How do you know its early sixteenth century?" I asked, feigning devotion to his every word. I moved closer and peered in, hoping he hadn't noticed my near comatose state.

He seemed startled that I was still here, probably because it had taken me so long to answer.

"I think it's early sixteenth century because of the border. Borders came into being in the late fifteenth century and in the early sixteenth century they looked like this one. They had lots of floral designs, although I do see some other symbols here including birds and plants. I'm not sure what those are about. Some of them seem rather odd for a border of that time." His hand moved about over the top of the tapestry to point to items of interest.

"And did I hear you say it was Flemish?" I wanted to stay in the game. Clearly I knew little about tapestry. Not a lot of them emerge on the Southern California art scene, and the Newport Art Theft Detail was not swimming with notices of thefts of 500-year-old textiles.

"I believe so. This mille-fleur design with the garden surrounding the animals is a design that was common in Bruges in the early sixteenth century," he said, scratching at new beard growth I had just noticed. He pointed again at the tapestry, though the whole thing looked like woven green leaves to me.

"How do you know this is from Bruges?" I asked. I

sounded as if I was challenging his expertise, but it wasn't intentional.

"I don't. It's an educated guess because of the subject matter in the foreground." He took a quick look at the front and back of the tapestry.

He caught me watching him. "What are you looking for?" I asked. I wanted to know everything so as to get ahead of this situation now that I was wide awake again.

"I'm looking for a mark I don't think would be there, and it isn't. In 1544, there was an edict that a weaver's mark had to be woven into tapestries. By 1547, Bruges tapestry-makers created a mark involving a gothic B with a crown above it. Later a broche or weaver's shuttle for the high warp loom was added. I see no such mark here. So again, I'm guessing this was done in the early sixteenth century before 1547," he finished.

He stood up over the table while stretching his back and rubbing his neck. He had been peering at this tapestry for hours now. His stomach was rumbling, and he suddenly complained of being tired and thirsty. I realized that I was too.

"I know you're in a great hurry, Detective Claire, but if I don't eat you may see the really grumpy side of me. Did you say you would go for Italian?"

The phone beeped in my purse. *Oh no.* I whacked a palm to my head.

"I forgot I have to have dinner with my parents tonight. My sister Annette just reminded me. I have to go." I grabbed my keys and ran for the door, nearly skidding on the wooden floor.

"Good, I'll go with you. I'm starving," Mark announced.

"No, you can't go. You wouldn't like it. I mean, it would be very weird." I stopped in the doorway with an outstretched hand like a school guard's stop sign. *No way. He was not coming.* I looked about the room wildly to see if there was anything I could use to help me make up a plausible excuse.

"Why not? I'm starving. Is your mother a good cook?" I could see he was being intentionally dense. *Damn, this wasn't funny.*

"Yes, but..." I felt true terror in my gut, like I had just become aware of an avulsed nail. He was not going. No way. I wasn't up to allowing him to witness the family dynamic quite yet—or ever. The room felt hot.

"What, you have strange parents?" Mark persisted. "Are they bad cooks? Poor dressers? Incarcerated? Mimes?"

"Yes. They're quirky. Bad quirky, not good quirky." I said quickly, looking apologetic while feeling stupid and deflated.

"Same as mine. Come on. Get your bag. I'll follow you in my car."

I saw him grab a jacket as he retreated, and I swear there were elbow patches.

CHAPTER NINETEEN

Claire and Mark at Dinner

Three hours of dinner crept by. Mark smiled and kept up with the family banter. But then, he didn't know what I knew.

I had been on the receiving end of dad's emotional traps more often than I could count. So had Annette. We were his "silly girls." Whether it was resentment, criticism or failed expectation, he had been there to let his girls know how they had been judged and found wanting because they weren't boys. We were hopelessly flawed by merely being female—genetically mutant, lacking a Y chromosome.

Annette's husband, who had died in Iraq, escaped Jim's scrutiny when he was alive. Or maybe it was the Y chromosome. That chromosome was a powerful thing. Dad was a coward who only attacked those he thought wouldn't attack back. Wasn't that the definition of a bully?

Annette announced that it was storytelling time for my nephews, Carson and Will, ages four and six. I put as many scatological references as I could into my invented tale of the "green bean boy"—my nephews' favorite character. A boy shaped like a green bean. I had even begun to believe that the green bean boy was a pretty cool dude.

I noticed that Mark watched from the edge of the hallway near the bedroom door. Annette was behind him. I could hear them whispering.

"Claire tells the best stories," I heard Annette say while the boys were "euw-ing" over a disgusting story tidbit I had thrown in for effect.

"Does she?" Mark asked. Annette nodded.

Mark seemed to be staring at me, but maybe he was staring at the boys' poster of The Hulk. All things green seemed to appeal to them, except vegetables.

The boys stopped listening and were running around the room imitating the green bean boy.

Annette continued, "My sister is oddly shy, though she's got the capacity to kick the shit out of most of the men we know."

Thank you Annette. That should make any man wild with desire.

I could feel Mark watching me. His eyes were glued to me like Silly Putty on shag carpet.

I finished the story in a ridiculous manner; the green bean boy fell into the sewer and would have to be rescued in the next tale.

"That's it boys. Next time you can find out how the green bean boy felt about riding diapers in the sewer like a ship on the ocean." The boys shouted another "EUWW!" as I gave them an air kiss.

We bade my parents and Annette au revoir. Mark walked me to my car, half-turning to wave good-bye to my family silhouetted in the doorway. I had to admit they looked sweet and harmless back-lit in the door frame by warm amber light.

"Your dad is interesting," Mark said. "You look just like him, Detective Claire. It's all there. Tall, thin, fierce eyes, and short, dark hair—of course, it looks much better on you."

Compliments—they made me feel anxious and uncomfortable. It had always been this way. I wanted to deny them before they left the other person's mouth, but I accepted Mark's compliments by practicing my confident, secure and graceful lady act.

"Thank you," I said and had the good sense to shut up.

We walked to the car. The night was chilly and foggy, and the smell of jasmine rose up from white-blossomed bushes. I had a millisecond of sheer gratitude. A brief moment of absolute pleasure rolled through me. Stomach full, nephews in bed, being on the receiving end of a compliment, and having just made a successful job of escaping dad's criticism and cruelty allowed me to ride high. Life was good—if I didn't count Nora.

"You did a nice job with your nephews. They seem to appreciate a sick sense of humor. When you said you would back over them with the car if they didn't shut up and go to sleep—you were kidding, right?"

"Yes," I laughed.

He opened my car door but for some reason entered the passenger seat after seeing me safely to my seat, even though we had driven in separate cars. *Hmm. He was confused. This was my car. I was going home.*

There was fog on the windshield. I didn't feel ready for where this conversation with Mark might go. I turned on the windshield wipers with enough torque to rip the wiper control from the steering column.

"You're afraid of him, aren't you?" Mark asked quietly. I stopped and looked at the windshield for a long time.

"Afraid?" I said. This was heading in a very personal direction—I looked out at the blackness beyond the car. "No, I'm not." I turned to look him in the face, but I swallowed hard.

Mark said nothing. I thought about his remark for a moment and turned my face away.

"Well, yes," I capitulated. "I guess I'm afraid he'll make his ten thousandth proclamation of disapproval towards me in front of a stranger, or even friends, just like he did tonight."

"No, I don't think that's what you're afraid of," he challenged.

"No? Well *doctor*, since you know my family so well after only three hours, tell me what you think I'm afraid of," I said with far more sarcasm than intended.

"I think you're afraid you'll believe him."

Chapter Twenty

Beatrice Follows Ardonne

I decided to follow Ardonne as he left the tapisserie. His threats to drown me and my Father would not be tolerated.

I pulled my cape around me and put the heavy hood over my hair. The evening was very cold. Breath steamed around my hood as I watched to see which way he headed. The tapisserie was near the home of our most famous painter of the past—Jan van Eyck.

I caught sight of Ardonne walking east toward the Herberghe Vlissinghe Pub.

I kept behind at a safe distance by walking along the canal the short length to the pub, passing the houses with stepped gable roofs while pressing myself against them so as not to be seen. I stepped carefully on the cobblestones to avoid dislodging them or striking my feet on a wine barrel.

How dare he threaten us! First my beautiful sister was taken away—my lovely, brilliant sister. Now he was threatening my Father and me. I would not bear such abuse.

Behind the pub Ardonne met another man, but it was too dark to discern his identity.

Sounds carried from inside the pub where men enjoyed their ale. I peeked through the window into the interior of the pub, where pale yellow walls above and warm brown wood below surrounded the warmth of the blazing fireplace. No one could see me. I walked near the back of the pub to watch the two men.

From nearby dark houses, pale gold patches of wavy light showed that fires and candles were lit inside. Many windows were covered with lace. Cooking smells wafted to me from the chimneys. These were probably homes where families were intact, where thick soup was being ladled into wooden bowls, and sisters laughed together while their parents ate contentedly. I shivered, alone in the dark, cold seeping into my shoes on the hard stones.

Now I could identify the other man. It was Monsignor Bernardo! But it was difficult to hear what they said. Here they both were—both of my enemies in one place! I walked closer, careful to step quietly along the cobblestones while pushing back my hood to hear.

"She must be eliminated—her Father also. The risk is too great. Make haste. You must do it before the week ends," Father Ardonne spoke in a low, harsh tone. He seemed to be the one in command, ordering a minion.

"Eliminated? How? You don't think I can do such a thing, do you?" Father Bernardo whispered.

Ardonne struck Bernardo hard on the face. I could hear the crack of his hand. I pulled back in the shadows, surprised by his ire.

"You cockroach!" he whispered as Monsignor Bernardo covered his cheek, rubbing the injury. "Now you are a coward? You weren't quite so reticent when fornicating with the older sister! Listen, I can have you named cardinal if you will simply listen to me. In a few years I can even have you replace his holiness, Pope Leo the Pustulant—that damned, miscreant windbag Giovanni de´ Medici!"

"But it must be done before he spends all the de´ Medici wealth: my family's gold florins. You will win the papal seat only with my help, and you will then return the gold florins the de´ Medicis have hidden after they stole them from my family." I could see spittle flying into Monsignor Bernardo's face.

Bernardo took a step back, shaking his head. "But if I am the pope, Philippe, you can hardly expect that I will be required to give you access to the papal treasury or that I will do your dirty work."

Ardonne struck Bernardo's face again with a hard smack and the fat Monsignor took a knee. This time it took him longer to recover his equanimity, and Ardonne kicked him hard in the side while Bernardo retched over the cobblestones.

"Do not pretend to have the intelligence to ascend to the papacy without my influence, you cretinous leech," I heard

Ardonne whisper as he pulled Bernardo to a standing position. He spoke with their noses nearly touching.

"Leo the Pustulant spends our florins on banquets and young boys, the addled sodomite that he is," Ardonne nearly spat the words.

"And now he has thousands more florins from indulgences, and chases after that twittering Wittenberg monk, Luther, to distract everybody from the mockery he has made of the Church in Rome. To distract everybody from the wealth His Holiness has poured into St. Peter's Basilica."

"Perhaps you are mistaken, Philippe? I understand the Church is penniless," Bernardo asked while backing away from Ardonne. The Monsignor did not seem so imposing now.

"My priapic friend, my family went bankrupt when the de' Medicis closed the Bruges bank forty years ago. They took all the family money. And since that time my family has lived like paupers. Can you imagine what this means?"

Ardonne raged on, "They have used my family's wealth to live like kings and to beget a pope. They hide the florins at the Vatican, and the Pope makes a pretense of being bankrupt. It ends now, with you and me. You, who cannot keep his cock in his cassock—what a fool I have chosen to do my bidding. Remember, without me you would not be Monsignor and will never be cardinal or pope."

Pope? Ardonne had the power to make the Monsignor a cardinal and pope? Surely this could not be true. Was the entire Church made of such men? We must all be fools to put our faith in such flawed flesh. Money would pay for the highest office in the Church?

Ardonne seemed to tower over the Monsignor now as the fat one was bent in dejection, "With me, Pope Leo's health will take a sudden turn for the worse. You will become cardinal, then pope, and assign me to the office of the treasury. You will frolic with your little boys and girls and I will have my florins. It is that simple. Even your addled mind can comprehend that, or perhaps I give you too much credit."

Bernardo bent his head and whispered something I could not hear. They walked away from the pub toward the canal.

As I came out of the shadows to follow, my shoe overturned a small cask behind the pub. Both men turned to look directly at me.

CHAPTER TWENTY~ONE

Nora Pleads

Davies was right about my reaction to old criticism,
but I thought he should mind his own business. I
needed him for 48 more hours, then we would go
our separate ways. I only needed to be accommodating for
two more days. I let him know I was ready to get back to the
business of the tapestry by pointing to the car door handle.

"Of course, I could be wrong, I have been many times
before," Davies capitulated politely while holding up both
palms, but making no move to leave the car.

"Yes, you are."

"Okay," he continued, as I gripped the steering wheel
and stared into the street, "in my home of origin we had
a different type of family craziness. It was the response to
money—at times generous and at other times miserly. It
plagued me until I decided to do what the Victorians did."

I took a deep breath. "Okay, I'll bite." Then I could go
home and pet Leila. "What did the Victorians do?" I asked
without enthusiasm.

"They placed the things they didn't understand, like dead
fetuses attached at the chest, into 'cabinets of curiosity.'

People could parade by and look at them when they wanted to, but the curiosities remained in the museum when everybody went home. They didn't have to be troubled by the curiosities or even understand them. It provided an odd kind of acceptance, or denial, I guess."

"So, I should lock my parents in a cabinet?" I asked.

Davies laughed and put his head back on the seat, looking out the skylight to the dark and damp night sky. "Something like that. I prefer to think of it as a safe house for the soul."

Perhaps there was more to this man than met the eye. There might be something like wisdom and a sense of humor, or even a sense of valor.

I still wanted to go home. I wasn't quite ready for the cabinet yet.

"I'm rambling," he said and grabbed the door handle.

"You are. I have a long day tomorrow," I said. I watched him leave the car and wave a cheery goodbye at me. I assumed that he was on his way to his own home, or safe house, wherever that was.

I headed once more up PCH toward my tiny apartment, thinking of the evening and of Mark's last comments. This wasn't the time for introspection. Maybe he was right, but I need to focus on Nora. My mind wandered back to the ground zero discussion Mark had started. Though he didn't know it, this was the Chernobyl of my memories.

That's one of the reasons Nora was so important to me. She knew my past and the shame I felt, but she was there for me. Since words rarely sufficed, she often said nothing when I shared.

Dad looked innocent enough, but he had been physically and emotionally abusive to Annette and me as children while mother looked on. Years passed with this behavior being repeated whether he was sober or drunk. During school years, my esteem sunk so low I looked for approval where I could find it.

When I thought of the young girl I had been, I wanted to weep for the loss of that girl's innocence: the one whose face would be slapped so hard by her own Father that a hand-shaped red mark would remain for hours, and the one who was so pathetically desperate for approval she would befriend those incapable of giving friendship.

Years of therapy had healed some of my and Annette's wounds. Nora had been there to listen. Slowly I had built a life of esteem and value. However, like an impressive work of architecture with a defect in the foundation, it could tumble down with the right stressors.

To revisit these memories was like accidentally looking at the sun. There was searing pain and instant withdrawal. It was to be avoided at all costs.

The fog obscured the sight of what would have been a moonlit night where the light would catch the cresting edge of the waves breaking on the rocks north of Laguna Beach, setting off white light against the black ocean.

I passed the charming public plot, Sherman's Garden, on my left. On warm summer days Nora and I would eat lunch outside in the garden, watching water spray over a bronze statue of a crane as we were surrounded by blooming, blue agapanthus. Tonight the garden was dark and tranquil.

I turned onto Dahlia, then to Begonia, where my loft and bed beckoned. I was beat. Dinner with the parents was excruciating, Mark's journey into my soul was unwelcome, and Alita Hansen would be badgering Simon to fire me as soon as she realized I had taken the tapestry.

I pulled into the garage under the loft, locking the car. There was a faint rustling sound that I dismissed as the wind. When the garage door came down, I smelled an unfamiliar herbal scent.

I entered the dark alley briefly to unlock the ivy-covered gate. Fog played with sound, making the nearby ocean noises mix with the scraping sounds of footsteps—somebody else's footsteps.

My mouth went dry. I could see shortened puffs of my breath in the fog. I reached back for my holstered gun, but my heel caught the edge of the sidewalk where the automatic sprinklers had turned the ground to mush. I fell back into the hedge and the figure moved closer.

"Stop right there!" My voice was tinny and loud, but the gun was steady in my hand.

"Oh get over yourself, Claire, it's just me," Nora answered. She stood over me while I extricated my shoe from the mud.

"Shit, you scared the hell out of me Nora!" I rubbed my ankle. My pants were muddy and my heels lopsided.

"Well can I come in?" she demanded. She looked grumpy and disheveled. Her hands were stuck firmly in jacket pockets as if to protect herself from unwanted touch.

"Uh, of course—come on. Sorry I yelled at you, and uh,

pulled a gun on you." I turned the key in the door and led Nora up the steps to my loft. Leila jumped at the top of the steps, not bothering to come down, since it was only Nora.

I threw the keys on the entry table as Nora flicked on the lights and sat on the couch. She didn't look happy. Why should she?

"Would you like some tea?" I sounded like a ludicrously formal butler. Nora could, and usually would, make her own tea. She nearly lived here.

"No. I'm not here for tea. Listen, you have to fix this right away, Claire. This morning when you took Paolo into custody, I thought you had to be kidding. I thought it was a joke, like those singing telegram things. I thought you and Artie would drive around the block, come back after five minutes to tell me how funny my face looked when you read him his rights."

Nora leaned forward to straighten the candlestick on the low wooden coffee table, ever the designer, even in her misery. She sat back and sighed, putting her fingers up to her lips to keep her trembling mouth still.

Her voice became high and cramped. "But you didn't come back. I waited for a long time. I sat in the kitchen and finished my drink. I took a shower. I laughed at first after I got over being sick to my stomach. By the time the shower was over, I wasn't laughing any more. It's not funny now. I want you to fix it. Now!" She gave me a beseeching look.

"I want to fix it too, Nora. And I will. I have the tapestry. I'm having an expert look at it. We'll figure it out. We'll find a basis for Paolo's claim." I sounded desperate, but it was her fault I went to that stupid party.

"Paolo's claim? You say that like you don't believe him. This is all a mistake. You don't know him. You want to look good for Simon so you can make the arrest, close the case, show him what a sharp woman he left behind, make him suffer."

"No. You can't believe that. You think I would do that?" I was stunned that she could attribute such a motive to me.

"I didn't think you'd ever take it this far. That's all. I'm appalled." She moved the candlestick again. Her voice was dull. Her blond hair, usually swept up playfully, hung and stuck to her face in fog-damp, limp tendrils. She hadn't taken her jacket off.

"Nora, I..." before I could finish, Nora stood and moved to the top of the staircase. I could see she was crying as she glanced back at me, before walking down the stairs and slamming the door.

I called out over the iron railing as she exited, "Please don't go. We can work on this together. Come back!"

The door re-opened. Nora's head appeared at the bottom of the steps. I looked down over the railing.

She said, "You know Claire, here's what's so ironic. You are so afraid of betrayal since Simon, but now you are the betrayer." She left and I sat down, one hand still holding the rail over the empty staircase.

Chapter Twenty-Two

Violence

They had seen me. The two priests looked in my direction. I flattened myself to the stone wall.

"Who is it? Who is there?" Father Ardonne shouted. Both men ran in my direction.

I stepped directly in front of them but dodged to the side, running. I could almost feel their hands upon my neck. Would they strangle me? Rape me? Throw me in the canal? The pounding in my ears obscured the sounds of their steps.

The men had the advantage of longer strides, but I was faster.

I ran through the tiny alley next to the pub, no wider than a horse, and hid in the shadows under the bridge at St. Annarei canal. My breath came quickly. I put my cape over my mouth, afraid the vapor from my breath might betray my hiding place.

They were on the bridge above me, whispering loudly, and their voices carried in the cold night air. The canals smelled particularly dank as I hid. Perhaps the wind was blowing their fetid smell my direction. I could hear water lapping quietly against the walls of the canals.

Ardonne's voice was wild. "Find her, you leech!" he said to Monsignor Bernardo. "This is your doing! Find her or I will find some other lickspittle to put in the papacy. Go!"

"And when you find her, kill her. Throw her in the canal and take care of the rest of them at the tapisserie," he continued to shout in his mad voice.

I planned to wait under the bridge until they both left. I could go to the Poorters Loge, for my Father knew merchants there. Or, I could run to the hospital. Perhaps they could hide me there.

I heard retreating footsteps but dared not look out. I waited a long time before I came out. I peered carefully around the underside of the bridge and saw nothing.

Then a large, rough hand grabbed my neck and lifted me until my toes dragged along the cobbles. I sputtered, but no breath came in or out. I could smell the onions and cabbage on his breath.

The strong hand squeezed hard on my neck as I was thrown into the stinking canal—the cold, dark waters soaking my heavy skirts, taking me down the frigid path to death.

Chapter Twenty Three

Claire and Mark at the Museum

Morning brought another bright, eye-searing blue sky without clouds. The trip to the museum was uneventful, but my mind was restless. I made it to the museum exactly when Mark Davies said he would be arriving.

I parked around the side and could smell the morning scents of eggs, coffee and jasmine from the flowered path that led behind the museum to a Mexican restaurant. Knowing we had a busy day, I had called in an order from my car. I brushed past the jasmine-covered, wooden fence along the precipice situated over the Pacific Ocean to pick up breakfast for the two of us.

I pressed the buzzer at the museum door. Fortunately Susan Price opened the museum door, and I headed to the office upstairs with my hands full.

Mark was already at it. Head down over the tapestry he said, "Ah, good to see you, good morning. Detective, see these?" As he gestured to the tapestry, he looked up again to see the bag in my hands, "Oh you brought breakfast." He appeared relieved and rubbed his hands together.

"I did. Here." I placed everything on his chair, assuming he could help himself. I knew from past treks to the restaurant that the food actually smelled better than it tasted.

He grabbed a coffee, blew on it and took a tentative sip while pointing to various birds and plants in the border. I saw a leopard, monkey, orange tree, crow, butterfly, strawberries, violets, and glass—in short, a slew of natural representations that meant nothing to me.

"Yes, are those unusual? Do they mean something?" I asked. I didn't feel stupid, I just felt frustrated at my inability to move this case forward independently. I was glad to be here and thrilled to have an expert at hand, but impatient for progress.

While he sipped his coffee, he provided information. "They are unusual. I'm thinking this tapestry belongs to a time period when the borders were rather predictable. There were leaves, flowers, and occasionally some Latin words. Later borders became more ornate. Eventually they looked like picture frames, but that was a much later time period."

He continued, pointing to specific areas of the tapestry border, "But this border has some symbols I don't usually see in a verdure—this type of tapestry. Look—see the leopard surrounded by violets, then there's a monkey of some kind in an orange tree, around this side there's a crow and then a butterfly. Over here are strawberries winding around something that looks like an orb of glass."

His arms moved while pointing to various woven symbols

I found difficult to discern. I looked where he pointed. All the symbols were entwined within vines and leaves in such a manner that made them nearly invisible, as they had been to me the day before.

"So, it all means what?" I asked again. I had a stirring of excitement. Surely he must have an idea about what this all added up to reveal. I wanted him to put together the clues so I could put down the coffee, get in the car, and get Paolo out of custody.

"Not sure," he said. I felt deflated.

"I have a book on symbols. Reach over to that bookshelf on your left, would you please? It's purple, see it there? Small one, the author is Ferguson. Oh also, there's one in that cabinet, see the dark green edge? Get that one too, please."

I perused the shelf, being cautious not to disrupt piles of books and papers. The shelves appeared to be in some sort of order but were packed to maximum capacity.

I handed over the books, looked down at my shoes, then cleared my throat and began, "You know what you were saying last night when we were in the car?" I didn't like venturing into this territory, but it was where we left off last night, and things still felt slightly uncomfortable.

"I know, that was rude," he said. He looked up at me and gave me a sheepish smile. "Sorry. It was, uh, I was out of line. Sometimes I fall in love with the sound of my own voice."

"Don't we all?" I said, "No, you were right." Admitting it felt better. Somehow saying "you were right" was easier than "I was wrong."

He seemed to sense my discomfort and interjected, "Your dad feels judged so he gives out judgment. He then feels it coming back at him again, and the cycle goes on and on." He stood quietly, waiting for me to process this.

"Uh huh," I replied. I was so accustomed to dismissing my father's behavior that I had rarely given myself over to thinking it through. The effect his behavior had on Annette and me was obvious, but I had never wanted to ask myself why he was the way he was.

"Okay. Last thing on the subject and then we study tapestry until we're blind," Mark said. "It's a cycle you *can* step out of."

That was a lot to digest and way too brief to be a plausible solution to a life-time problem. I looked at Mark. He looked troubled.

"What?" I asked. I didn't intend to be obtuse, but I really couldn't get my brain to engage in this.

"Nothing. Why don't you get some cotton gloves, and we'll go over this inch by inch." He squared his shoulders. I did as I was directed. I was glad to let this conversation drop.

It took us most of the day. Mark looked up the meaning of the symbols, and I wrote them on the white board.

Sometimes he gave me a task, which was mainly looking up obscure references in tapestry tomes. The cool spring morning had turned into a hot afternoon, and the museum air conditioner labored overtime to keep the room cool.

At 3:30, we both looked up to the white board. Its bulleted points read:
- mille-fleur tapestry
- Bruges? early sixteenth century?
- center scene an enclosed garden with animals—typical

- no weaver's mark on back or front—woven prior to 1544
- leopard lying among violets
- monkey sitting in orange tree
- crow eating butterfly
- strawberries appear to be twining around glass
- border symbolism (not the usual twining leaves)
  - leopard symbol: devil, antichrist, adultery
  - violets symbol: humility and Virgin Mary
  - monkey symbol: evil, the devil, heresy
  - orange tree
    - tree symbol: life (with leaves), death (no leaves)
    - orange tree symbol: purity and chastity
  - crow symbol: death, devil, misfortune
  - butterfly symbol: soul, death, resurrection
  - strawberries symbol: innocence and humility, righteousness
  - glass symbol: purity

Our eyes moved over the white board. We looked at each other dispiritedly. I was starving. My eyes hurt. I rummaged in my bag for eye drops.

Mark spoke first. "All right, let's go over what we know. The tapestry was commissioned by a duke. Where was he from again, by the way?"

I looked at my notes. "Florence."

"Florence," he repeated. "So he sends an envoy to Belgium to have this made. Bruges is the likely spot for a mille-fleur at that time, though things declined later in the century for complicated reasons."

He continued. "This is a mille-fleur. This is an early sixteenth century mille-fleur. But it has odd borders. I know I'm repeating myself, but I have to say it out loud to see if anything adds up. Did you notice these odd partial lines at the very edge of these two borders?"

"Where?" I look where he pointed. Indeed, there were short segments of lines at odd angles to one other. They appeared random and meaningless, but he was right in that they didn't look like the wavy lines of the vines or flowers.

"Looks to me like someone started something and then had a change of mind," I said.

"Yes it does. Except look down this side and the opposite side. There are several of these straight lines and some curved lines. These aren't parts of a vine or leaves. They almost look to me like mending, but they're not." He fingered the edges of the tapestry with his white-gloved hands.

"Mark, I'm sorry but I have to get a snack and take a break before my head falls off from leaning over this thing. Look, you stay at it while I run back to the restaurant for afternoon snacks. I'll bring you another coffee." I grabbed my bag, not waiting for his response.

My head was aching. At this point I was bored senseless. How could he look at this nonsense for so long? I had a case to solve and a tapestry to return to the evidence room. I had a friendship to rescue. I was running out of time.

I could hear him talking to me, voice elevated, as I neared the hallway, "You know, symbols were the way they told stories back then because nobody could read." However, I had already escaped into the fresh, yet warm afternoon ocean breeze.

My cell phone rang as soon as I was on the sidewalk to

the back side of the building. It was Artie.

"Are you nuts?" I heard him ask.

"Probably. What do you mean exactly?"

He pressed on rapidly as I smelled the fishy ocean air. "Alita Hansen had a stroke after she realized you took evidence, and she told Simon to fire you. The guy from the Vatican is on a plane. His name is," he hesitated, struggling with pronunciation, "Signore Piero DiAlberto. And I'm wondering if they'll make me partner up with Marjorie Wells after you get canned—you know I can't stand her! And could you explain why I'm on the outside of all of this?"

I took a deep breath, sitting on a tree stump outside the Mexican restaurant. "Sorry Art. I feel like I shouldn't put your career at risk. This isn't your battle. And Marjorie might let you sniff her hairspray, or even use it, if you're real nice to her."

"DeMaer, let me help. You know I hate change. You're weird, but you're my partner. Let me do something," he pleaded.

We had been working together for several years and had fallen into a comfortable partnership. Artie was senior to me in the chain of command, but he had difficulty speaking easily with strangers so I would often take the lead. I missed him. I missed his insights. We usually reviewed case details in the car during ever-present traffic jams.

"I didn't know that there was so much to be done," I answered. "Can you stall DiAlberto? Pick him up at the airport and get lost or something? And Artie, can you call Nora?" This last request was one from a real weasel, and I knew it.

"Oh no. *No.* I'm not calling Nora," Artie protested.

"Just see if she can meet me at the apartment tonight," I asked.

Then I felt it. That odd, but unmistakable feeling. My knees were shaking. The plants hanging on poles overlooking the ocean's scenic walk were swaying. Car alarms were all sounding at once. I shouted into the phone, "Earthquake!"

Chapter Twenty-Four

A Rescue

Strong hands gripped my bodice, pulling at it as I sank lower into the canal. I felt the laced bodice tear as I was lifted out of the water, a strong hand squeezing one breast. Cold water exploded from my nostrils as I surfaced. A figure pulled at my skirts, tearing them off. I desperately sucked in breaths and then vomited sea water.

My body fell to the cobblestones, and my face was angled into a puddle where I was sick over and over again. I was too weak to lift my nostrils out of the vomitus. The figure wrenched at the wet bottom of my kirtle, but I was too feeble to resist.

There was a man next to me, but I could not lift my head to distinguish him. Perhaps he would stab and ravish me now as he was pulling at my clothes.

He turned me over. I was too breathless to cover my exposed breasts and sodden undergarments.

It was the Duke! He took off his velvet jacket and

placed it around me. All his words came out in a rush as he cradled my head. "I followed you. I was outside in the garden when your visitor came to the tapisserie. I apologize, but I followed. I do not know why. I saw them throw you in the canal!"

"Beatrice, what is going on? You must let me help you."

I started to shiver great, racking shivers. My teeth clamped together. I could not answer then even if I had wished to do so.

He eventually lifted and carried me toward home, but I put my hand out, "No, no it is not safe. Please, please send a message to my Father. It is not safe for him." Speaking through teeth clamped shut with cold was difficult.

He took me instead to his lodging, calling for a servant as we entered. Both of them placed me on a bed with wool blankets atop me. The servant brought warm wine while the Duke remained near the bed.

"Here. Drink this," the Duke said. "I will arrange for you to stay here, and I will take another room. First, I must go to your house to warn your father." He stood to leave.

I reached out a naked arm from under the warm blankets and held the warm skin of his wrist while saying, "Thank you, Excellency. Thank you. You saved my life. How can I thank you?"

"I do not know the full extent of your troubles, Beatrice, but I fear that you have taken on a power much greater than you can handle. I beg you to reconsider your actions. Marie would not want you to join her so soon in heaven."

CHAPTER TWENTY FIVE

Claire Frees Mark

I dropped the cell phone. The swaying stopped, but then the hard jerking started. There were two large jolts. Car alarms continued to blare. My hands shook, but not from the earthquake. I watched the museum creak and sway slightly. The building's security alarm whooped wildly.

As the ground movement abated, I moved toward the entrance to help those inside. Suddenly the glass entrance doors shattered into pieces that fell to the ground like snow in a globe. Though I was nowhere near the glass, I instinctively put my hands over my head and eyes.

When the glass stopped falling I remembered that Mark was in the building, along with Susan and Roy. I ran into where the glass door had been and stepped over the glass shouting, "Roy! Mark! Susan!"

I ran upstairs calling their names. Mark's office was in shambles, papers and books strewn everywhere. I couldn't see Mark, Susan or Roy. The suspended lights were still swinging wildly to and fro, creaking in complaint.

"Roy! Mark! Susan!" I called again as I stepped over piles of books and papers. Huge bookcases had fallen, probably under the weight of so many texts, and I stepped over them calling out. In fact, I realized all the bookcases were now on the floor.

And there it was: a bloody face, under one of the bookcases—Mark's face, with the tapestry rolled next to him. He must have tried to save it.

"Oh, no, no, no! Mark! Mark!" He didn't move. Blood covered his face, leaking from his mouth.

I bent to the floor and put my hands between the bookcase shelves. I touched his cheek. My fingers came away covered in red, but his cheek was warm. He moaned and moved slightly. He was alive!

"Mark, Dr. Davies, are you, uh, can you move? Are, oh, can you hear me?" I tried to move my hands within the bookcase shelf in a helpful way, but there was little space around his face.

His lips moved gingerly. Blood bubbled over his teeth. "I think I'm okay. Was that an earthquake? I think I just have a split lip and, my uh, are my teeth broken?" He gave me a wan smile and tried to show me his blood-covered teeth.

Odd as it seems, everyone in California wonders if they've just been in an earthquake when it's the only obvious answer. Since we're all accustomed to the Earth being solid and unmoving, we just can't believe it when it all starts to move. It's as if the universe isn't obeying a basic law of physics, similar to the notion of objects falling up. The earth moving always strikes us as being out of the question. But when the shaking is over, everyone shouts out what they think the quake registered on the Richter Scale. *"That was a 6.5!"*

I looked carefully at his teeth covered with blood, "I don't know. They're all bloody."

Just then Roy came into the room, to my great relief. He saw me kneeling over Mark's bloody face.

"Hey man, are you all right?" he said, kneeling. "Let's get this bookcase off you. Kind of hard to tell if you're fine when you have a bookcase on your chest."

Amazingly, Roy seemed to have the strength of an Olympian. He lifted the bookcase while I pulled at Mark's legs and arms, not knowing which body part to touch. I was careful not to move his head or neck.

Mark made pained sounds but lifted his head and crawled out from under the bookcase to survey the damage to the room and to himself. Blood dripped from his face.

Roy's brows danced together, "Man, you look bad. Where do you hurt?" and then to me, "Oh, Detective, what about you?" He seemed finally to notice me in the room.

I replied I was fine, but stumbled a bit as I got up to step over the books on the floor.

Mark touched his lip, looked at his bloody fingers and noticed blood dripping onto his T-shirt. "I think it's just my lip and maybe my gums or tongue. I think a book fell on my face and forced my teeth through my lips. I can't tell. Are my teeth all there?" He looked to me. Apparently I would have to do the mouth exam. I didn't want to look.

I placed both hands carefully on the sides of his head, moved very close and peered into his mouth. I moved his lips aside gently with my fingertips to see if any teeth were missing. Blood was oozing from his gums, tongue and lips. With my face inches from his face, I felt the teensiest bit dizzy. "Looks bloody, but all your teeth are there," I pronounced.

I am not a sissy about blood. Annette and I used to play rough outside: riding bikes, falling, getting lacerated, getting up, fighting and falling again. *Why was I feeling giddy? Must have been the earthquake.* I hate earthquakes. *Another reason to move to Canada.*

Mark sputtered between thick lips, "That had to be a six." I laughed at the perfect Californian response to an earthquake.

"Mark, let me take you to the hospital," Roy said.

"I can do it Roy," I said. "Can you get someone to help move furniture back in place and see if you can pull the tapestry out of the mess?" It might take several someones because the room was a disaster. I hoped Roy wasn't the only other male employee available to help lift the bookshelves.

"Yeah. Let me call the guys in the warehouse. You go ahead, and watch out for aftershocks. I'll get Mark down the steps to your car." Roy held Mark around the waist, and they both began to pick their way over the fallen books. Just as he had mentioned aftershocks one came. The walls began to shake again, and car alarms starting going off again. The light fixtures waved to and fro. Roy and Mark stumbled to the wall and sat heavily next to it. I found my way next to them and waited it out.

"A four and a half," we said in unison when it ended.

By the time we reached my car most of the car alarms had finally stopped, and nothing appeared to be swaying. My least favorite memories after an earthquake are the swaying light fixtures and the sounds of pool water swishing against the sides of pools. I don't like the ways walls move either. Walls are meant to be still, but not on our edge of the tectonic plate.

I pulled the Mustang up to the broken glass door and Roy pushed Mark into the front passenger side, protecting his head like a cop. Mark had a bloody towel held to his mouth. "He'll probably bleed all over your car," Roy said, looking fondly at my Mustang.

"No problem," I said. Although I loved my car, I meant it. This man was helping me. He could bleed in my car if need be. I started the car and pulled onto PCH carefully while holding a hand in front of Mark's chest, as if I could stop him from any further harm.

The hospital wasn't far, and oddly there were few cars on this usually busy stretch of road. I guessed the earthquake had momentarily ceased all action.

"Should I ask you why you don't have the bookcases bolted to the walls?" I said. Probably not a very nice thing to say out loud to a man whose face had just been squashed.

"That was on my to-do list." He put his head back on the headrest and closed his eyes. I decided to stay quiet.

The Emergency Room was full, but since Mark looked bloodier than the rest he was brought back to a bed quickly.

That didn't mean he was seen quickly. He was triaged by a harried looking nurse, who must have decided it wasn't so bad after all. I sat with him, in a curtained-off area, while we watched white shoes and legs covered with green scrubs walk past the bottom of the dividing curtain. It felt like hours.

We fell into conversation, though I was doing most of the talking. Mark's mouth looked like he had fallen under a lawnmower.

I asked if he wanted some water, and he said he did. I leaned over the bed to lift the carafe of water, but an *ohh* sound came out of his mouth.

"Sorry! Did I lean on you?" I lifted up instantly, afraid I had pressed on some painful, unknown chest injury. I pulled my hands back and held them up high, as if a bank-robbery was in progress.

"No," he said, "you smell so good."

I started to laugh. I couldn't stop. Earthquakes do that. They make you giddy and glad to be alive. Sometimes after an earthquake I would sit outside looking at the trees and sky, just grateful to have one more day on the Earth. Then my laugh broke and I started to cry.

"I'm about to be fired, I've lost my best friend, we had an earthquake that nearly killed you, you have lips the size of kielbasas, and you think I smell good." Leaning forward I put both hands on my knees to support my weight as I laughed and cried.

He looked at me with the best smile his lips could manage and gave me a shoulder shrug.

"Yeah. That's about the long and short of it," he said. "Can't help myself. You just smell that good so I thought of kissing you, but now that I think about it, don't get near my lips." He waggled his hands to indicate I shouldn't come near.

I told him not only would I stay a safe distance from his lips, but also that he must have a serious head injury and be hallucinating. I also told him I needed to check my phone messages outside.

Outside it had turned into a beautiful night, clear and cool with faint ocean sounds and smells on the air. I watched cars come up the hill while checking my phone. Simon had called me at least seven times. Artie's phone was busy repeatedly. I listened to Simon's messages. All of them were the same: where was I, what the heck did I think I was doing, Alita was having a stroke, he was going to fire me, I had lost my mind, didn't I think about his career.

When I returned to Mark's bedside, a doctor was stitching his lip. Mark seemed very brave. I was sure the injections of lidocaine hurt more than anything else. He made some faces along with sharp intakes of breath during repeated injections, and I noticed his hands gripping the sheets. I put my hand over his since I had gotten him into this.

When the doctor finished, a nurse gave him instructions for observations related to his concussion. He should stay in bed. He should return if there was vomiting, worsened headaches or progressive loss of consciousness. I listened closely so I would remember the instructions for him.

Mark was released with black stitches on his lips looking like squashed spiders, and an icepack for his head. The lips had taken on a purple hue, with bloody ooze at the edges of the stitches.

"The doctor said I took a chunk out of my tongue and that's why there was so much blood."

He talked like Marlon Brando in *The Godfather*, and I felt genuinely sorry for him. However, I still needed him to work. I was running out of time. I was embarrassed to bring it up, but unless death was imminent I had to get him back to work while I still had the tapestry.

"Look," I said, "I'll get the tapestry. I'll take care of you at my apartment. We can continue to work on it if you feel well enough."

"Okay." He didn't argue, and he sounded tired. He was being awfully accommodating for a man who had lost part of his tongue.

"I'll call Roy—he can load it into my car when we drive past the museum."

I called ahead, and we met Roy at the museum. He mentioned that Susan and everyone else were fine. The bookshelves in Mark's office were apparently the most dangerous objects in the place, other than the glass doors. The museum had done a great job of placing museum wax in all the appropriate exhibits. Too bad they didn't think to wax Mark to the walls.

I reached Artie on my way back to my apartment while Mark snoozed in the passenger seat. He said, "DeMaer, I've been worried. You shouted 'earthquake' and then I don't hear from you for two hours. I thought you had fallen into the Pacific. I thought you were shark fodder."

I wasn't shark fodder. I told Artie what had transpired.

Since we were headed north on PCH to my apartment, the ocean appeared perfectly normal on my left side as I looked out the car window. One would never believe there had just been a tectonic event. It was almost as if it should have been expected a mountain, new island, or maybe even a volcano to have risen out of the ocean.

"But Mark— uh, Dr. Davies—has a nasty fat lip and

concussion. Can you meet us at my place? And Art, did you reach Nora?" I braced myself for the response.

"She's not too keen on the idea of seeing you or speaking to you, but I made it sound like she could help me on the case, so she relented. Nora will be by there later this evening."

I hung up as I pulled into the garage. I had called ahead to Maizie so I could have some help getting Mark up the staircase. Maizie is little, but strong. I also asked her to put Leila somewhere so that Mark wouldn't fall over her when he arrived.

Maizie and I helped Mark out of the car. "This is my neighbor, Maizie. She's also a premier dog-sitter," I introduced her with my best compliment. Maizie gave a wave and chattered constantly as we pushed and pulled Mark up the staircase.

With great effort we got him to the loft and placed him on the bed. He looked pale and exhausted. "I'll get you some water," I said as Maizie and I left the loft.

In the kitchen, I explained to Maizie what had happened. "Oh gosh," she said. "I thought you did that to him."

Chapter Twenty-Six

Safe Lodging

In the Duke's lodging house, I slept for hours under the warm woolen blankets. A servant brought clothes to me when I awoke. I did not recognize the clothing, but it fit. I descended to the sitting room near the fireplace on the street level to wait for the Duke or my Father.

In time the Duke returned. "Mejuffrouw van Hecke," he spoke softly and formally. He bowed with his beautifully long, straight leg forward and hands out, with one holding his cap. This disturbed me. It was not right for a Duke to bow to a craftsman's daughter. Nothing was right about this.

"Your Excellency, you have news of my Father?" It felt odd to be so formal with the man who had pulled me nearly drowned and half naked from the canal.

"Beatrice," his voice was softer and kind, "I could not find your father. Your home is silent. The tapisserie is full of workers, but no one knows of your father's disposition."

This was strange news. Father should be there. His

travels were over for some time. Antwerp had delayed many of his projects, and he vowed to stay at home. Other than visiting members at the guild hall, his purchasing trips were over, and he rarely went out. I bought the food. I purchased the wool. I went out for supplies. There was no reason for him to be absent.

The Duke continued. "And, I beg your forgiveness, but I must leave immediately to speak with my betrothed. There has been a complication." He spoke with his head down.

"How so, Your Excellency?" I asked. The warm room felt secure, but I heard notes of concern in the Duke's speech.

"After I pulled you from the canal and brought you to these lodgings, I met Father Ardonne in the street. He asked after your health. I explained about your unfortunate meeting and rescue from a pair of murderous jackals."

"Ardonne became very silent, inquiring if I was your protector and lover. It was an appalling question. I said you were a gentlewoman without blemish, and that it was preposterous to call a Duke the lover of a—well—I reproached him for his assumptions." The Duke appeared ill at ease. He did not wish to speak of the obvious differences in our society.

He continued, "Ardonne responded with great malice. He cautioned me to mind my business, and when I argued, he threatened excommunication. If this happens, Beatrice, I am ruined, and my marriage cannot go forward."

He repeated "If I am excommunicated, my family is ruined."

Chapter Twenty Seven

A Curious Finding

Maizie left us alone after she brought Leila up the staircase. I fetched Mark water that he sipped while complaining that his lips were awakening from the lidocaine, and the water felt like lye. I told him to rest on my bed, and that I would awaken him soon to make sure the concussion didn't cause a lack of consciousness.

Artie arrived once Mark had fallen asleep on my bed in the loft. He went to my car with me to get the tapestry. The day seemed calm, and the afternoon was cooling. This felt odd after the excitement of the earthquake. Many Californians claim that weather affects earthquakes (the Shake-and-Bake theory), but I was not among them.

"So, are you supposed to let him sleep? Aren't you supposed to check him because he has a concussion?" Artie asked as he heaved out an end of the tapestry from the car.

I told him I would awaken Mark every hour or so. If he seemed clueless, I would take him back to the emergency room as the nurse had directed.

We took the tapestry up the staircase and dropped it on my living room floor unceremoniously. Leila gave a start but otherwise stayed in her soft, plush bed shaped like a faux leopard, furry lima bean.

I asked if Simon had called Artie again. Artie said he had about every two hours and wondered aloud why I was being such an idiot. I had been ignoring Simon's calls. Simon knew where I was and what I was doing. He knew I had one day left. There was nothing I needed to say to him. I told Artie I was ignoring Simon, and though I caught a reproving look, he said nothing.

With the tapestry safely inside, Artie helped himself to a sandwich and ate it while half-sitting, half-reclining on my couch. We talked about the case. I cautioned him about pissing off Simon. This was my battle, not his. He ignored my comments. He asked how far Mark and I had gotten. I filled him in. I talked about where and when the tapestry was made, as well as what symbols it contained—basically all I knew from Mark.

"That doesn't tell us diddly," Artie complained, chewing loudly.

"I know. But what if the symbols mean something important? Mark says that's how they told stories in paintings and tapestries. Most people at the time couldn't read," I explained. "What if the symbols are why the Catholic Church wanted it?"

Artie reviewed the symbols aloud with me. Just then the doorbell rang. I hopped up to go to the door, but it creaked open and Nora made a tentative entrance up the stairs, allowing the cooling air and nascent fog to drift up the staircase.

"Hi," she called. It was a nervous, flat greeting without

friendship. She climbed the steps heavily.

"Hi. Come in." I gesticulated wildly to have her come up the steps and felt embarrassingly enthusiastic to see her.

She came up the staircase, and Artie took over—bless him. He thanked her for coming and filled her in on our progress, or lack thereof, before the earthquake. He motioned up the loft to indicate where Mark was resting.

She looked up at the loft and seemed furious, lips set in a line. She whispered to me, "You have no clue about the tapestry, and the curator is in your bed? How does this help, Claire?"

"He's not *in* my bed Nora, he's *on* my bed resting. He has a concussion and a fat lip, and he can probably hear us." I was beginning to feel edgy about her obvious resentment, and I certainly didn't appreciate the implication that I had been bedding Davies instead of following up on the case.

Artie ignored our interchange and went back to summarizing about the tapestry for Nora.

"I know about symbolism in tapestry," Nora said, surprising the two of us.

"You do?" both Artie and I chimed at the same time.

"I studied Renaissance art during design school. That was when perspective first appeared in art. We had to take various art classes but Renaissance art was my favorite. Show me the tapestry again."

Just as she said this, Mark appeared on the staircase. His short hair was flat on one side, and he had a slightly puzzled look on his face. His fat lips now looked like something out of the chariot race in *Ben Hur*.

I made introductions. Nora went into the ole charm

mode. Mark, Nora and Artie were all sitting on the floor around the tapestry and pointing before I knew it. They all started talking at once.

Mark reviewed, "All right, symbols of good and evil are here," he said as he pointed. "Evil is represented by the leopard, monkey, and crow," he gestured. "Good is symbolized with the violets, orange tree, butterfly, strawberries and glass. What does that tell us?"

We looked at each other, flummoxed. We looked at Nora.

"Maybe it reads from left to right like a book," Nora offered.

We stared at the tapestry, all heads moving from left to right. It started with the orange tree, then the monkey in the orange tree and the leopard lying among the violets. The next time the orange tree appeared, it was devoid of leaves. To the right, a crow captured a butterfly. Finally, there were strawberries twining around a glass orb.

Nora pointed to a tiny bird in the lower right corner that none of us had seen. "What kind of bird is this?" she asked.

Mark squinted and bent close to the weaving, "A nightingale," he replied.

Artie looked interested, and I caught his expression.

"You know something about nightingales, Art?" I asked.

"I'm thinking. There's a story in mythology—Greek, I think. It's not coming to me. It's in the back of my mind."

Mark bemoaned the fact that all his books were under a pile of rubbish in his office. Nora asked why we couldn't check the meaning on my computer. I attempted to investigate the meaning online, but only factual information about the bird was presented. I read it aloud from a research database:

"The nightingale is larger than a robin, 15-16 cm in length, plain brown with a reddish tail. *Blah blah*...so named because they sing at night," I finished.

Nora looked at me like I had thrown a dead puppy on the floor. "How is that helpful?" She turned to Mark and Artie for advice.

"Let's go over it again. Arthur, you tell us what you see, then Claire, then Nora. Maybe each of us will have a different idea," Mark proposed.

We each reviewed what we saw. Our thoughts ran along the same vein—some kind of situation involving good and evil in battle, with evil appearing victorious but good being the last image: the strawberries and glass orb. None of us had a clue about the nightingale.

Artie stretched and suggested food, though it seemed he just ate that sandwich thirty minutes ago. He lifted the tapestry unceremoniously off the floor to throw it onto the couch. Unfortunately, Leila had taken the couch by that time. Artie threw it on top of her, causing her to yelp and leap up, sending the tapestry to the floor.

It landed inner side down, Leila somehow under one end. She scrambled out, unharmed. Nora picked up both ends, right side of the image facing in, to roll it up and place it back in a safe spot. As she did so, she said, "Art, come here."

Her voice sounded low and curious. She pointed to the sides she had folded inward—the two horizontal sides of the tapestry.

"Those look like words," Artie said. He pointed to what Mark and I had seen on the edges before, but we had thought it might be mending in the border.

Mark moved quickly to stand next to Artie. "Show me," he said through swollen lips.

Artie put the sides of the tapestry together and showed him what now appeared to be words. When the sides of the tapestry were brought together, the hatch marks met to create a more understandable design in the form of odd looking words.

We all screamed and danced around like football stars in the end zone after a touchdown, but Mark looked back at the tapestry. Leila began to bark.

"Claire, get a mirror," Mark said.

I looked all over my bathroom and in my purse until finally Nora produced a mirror from her purse.

Mark held the mirror up to the words. The words were backward—in Latin.

Mark looked up at me while Artie said, "DeMaer, didn't you study linguistics in college?"

Chapter Twenty-Eight

The Duke

Ruined? Was it possible that by helping me, I had ruined the Duke's prospect of marriage, as well as his family's alliance with the Haghenbeek's land and wealth? If he could not marry in the Roman Catholic Church, his family would reject him—all of society would reject him. I knew this happened. While it seldom happened to simple people such as my own, religious ostracism usually targeted the powerful and wealthy, such as the Duke. Father remarked how easily the Church would excommunicate their members and sometimes torture or burn them.

This business had already ruined my sister, and now it harmed the Duke. I must speak with Father. He would advise me properly.

I could no longer stay in a warm lodging, while drinking hot wine by the fire. I must find Father to repair the damage I might have caused the Duke. Would his family even need the tapestry we had nearly completed if no marriage were to occur?

I left the lodging to search for Father. I walked west toward Jan van Eyck Place. In the distance a familiar figure walked toward me—Geertruyd. She stepped slowly, head down. As she grew closer, I was certain of her identity. I poked my arm out of the unfamiliar sleeve, giving a welcoming wave.

Geertruyd did not wave. She seemed breathless as she held out her hands to clutch mine. Her face was desperate; tears and mucous mingled beneath her nose. She rubbed it with her sleeve.

She grasped my fingertips to her lips and uttered, "Oh Beatrice, Beatrice. I must be the one to tell you. Your poor, dear father was found in the canal last night after you were rescued. He is—I, oh—he is murdered."

No, no, no. I told her she was mistaken. "Show me his body, show me!" I cried.

She took me to the guild where his body was temporarily placed. It was not him. It was not my Father. She was mistaken. The face was too swollen. The hands were not recognizable. The hair was swept over a wet brow, obscuring a purple face. This was not Father. Relief made me feel weak.

But, the man's cloak had red embroidery along the edges, similar to what Marie and I had stitched for Father's cloak. I remembered it because the thread was so expensive, Marie and I saved for months to buy it. The schaarlaken color was dear because it came from crushed, pregnant, female lice.

Geertruyd prayed aloud behind me, "Holy Mary, mother of God, pray for us sinners, now and at the hour of our death. Amen."

My shaking hands reached for the wet hair.

Holy Mary, mother of God, pray for us sinners, now and at the hour of our death. Amen.

My hands shook so hard that my arms and head moved as well.

Holy Mary, mother of God, pray for us sinners, now and at the hour of our death. Amen.

I moved the wet hair off the swollen face to expose it, and I saw the white-edged slash across the throat.

Holy Mary, mother of God, pray for us sinners, now and at the hour of our death. Amen.

I heard screaming. The voice was my own.

CHAPTER TWENTY~NINE

Latin Illuminates

"Intra, luscinia cantat," I struggled with the pronunciation of the Latin. I announced this to the assemblage as I read it in the mirror.

"What the heck does that mean?" Artie stared at me with a confused and exasperated expression.

"Oh! It means, 'within, the nightingale sings.'" I looked around, certain that someone would say "AHA!" and that all would be revealed.

The faces were intense, focused on mine. No one said a word.

"Within, the nightingale sings," I said again. "That's what it means."

Mark looked back to the tapestry, his shoulders slouched. "Claire, Nora, Art, I have no idea what that means. I just don't know. Maybe it's the concussion, but right now I don't have one thought. I'm sorry. I don't know how to help you. I wish I did." He held his head, and I knew he must be hurting.

Artie petted Leila. He looked around the room as if trying to find a distant thought, and then he began to shake a finger near his ear. "It's a myth. I know it. Claire, do you have any books on mythology? Greek mythology?"

Oddly enough, I did. In my bathroom, the book sat along with other books I read for six minutes daily. I figured like everyone else with books in the bathroom that in twelve years, *voilà*, the books would be finished.

I handed him the heavy, gold-edged book. Artie paged through it, reviewed the index, and paged again. Nora looked piqued, and I noticed one of her legs was shaking up and down. Artie made a *hmm* sound and then stopped at a page and slapped it. "That's it!" he announced. Nora started in fright when Artie hit the page.

He read, pointing to the entry,"...the ancient story of Philomela who is raped by her brother-in-law, King Tereus of Thrace. He then tears out her tongue."

We looked at each other, hands over mouths, saying aloud, "ooohhh." Mark looked especially pained and covered his stitches.

Artie continued, "Philomela is transformed into a nightingale, doomed to chirp out the name of her rapist for eternity." He looked up at all of us again, and we signaled him with the hand-rolling go-on sign. "Okay, but before she is turned into a nightingale, she gets her revenge by weaving a tapestry...revealing the facts of the rape." The last four words he spoke very slowly.

Mark looked at me. "A rape," he said. "This tapestry is about a rape."

Chapter Thirty

Beatrice's Losses

I stayed with Geertruyd for weeks, sleeping with her in bed each night. Her mother brought me soup, bread, porridge and fish, but I closed my eyes and refused to eat. Her father sat on the edge of the bed, asking if he could allow the guildsmen come in to speak with me about the disposition of my house and the tapisserie. I declined with the shake of my head.

I heard nothing from the Duke. Weeks passed without notice. Spring and then summer warmed the air in Geertruyd's small bed space that was surrounded by heavy drapes. I heard birds singing and muffled voices, as well as smelled flowers blooming and food cooking. None of it seemed to matter.

Geertruyd was kind and generous with me. Her cheerfully round face showed compassion when I rejected offers of bread and soup. I felt a sense of even greater pain for increasing Geertruyd's burden.

I began to get out of bed to help Geertruyd's mother with

the cooking and cleaning in repayment for her kindness, but I seldom spoke to anyone. My clothes hung from my frame as if they belonged to a different person—a larger and livelier person. That person no longer existed. I would remain diminished for life.

One day in mid-summer, Geertruyd asked if I would walk along the canals with her. There was to be a bell concert in the evening light. I was reluctant and made excuses, but she warmed me with her smile and offered to walk me past the most delicious smelling apricot buns on the way to the bell tower.

She held my arm as we walked to the bell tower square. The evening was warm with pink light fading behind the gabled roofs, as we approached the belfry. The gables looked like green and brown steps rising up to the clouds and back down.

"I have news, Beatrice," she said as we walked. "The Duke has sent word to me that he is in Bruges and would like to speak with you. He is waiting at the bell tower."

I looked at her, not comprehending. My thoughts had become so slow since Father's death. The Duke was away meeting his betrothed. I could not recall where at that instant.

"The Duke? After all these months? What does he want? The tapestry? It must be finished by now, the apprentices haven't stopped weaving," I replied. This was more than I had spoken in months.

We came upon the cloth hall and belfry square. I saw the familiar figure of the Duke, and we approached one another. I curtsied low and he bowed to me as if I were a queen, with an arm out to the side holding his cloak and one leg forward.

Geertruyd moved away quickly to purchase the apricot buns from a street vendor. I looked briefly at the Duke who seemed thinner, older and more tired. There was pain in his countenance. Pain was familiar to me. I could see a fellow traveler on this path of pain.

A slight breeze moved my skirt against my ankles, and I lowered my eyes in the Duke's presence. "Your Excellency, I hope you and your family are well. How may I be of assistance?" I kept my head low and bent at the waist.

"Mejuffrouw van Hecke, first may I express sincere sympathy upon the untimely and tragic death of your father. I received news of it on the road to Mechelen from a servant who had been staying in Bruges."

I kept my head down, nodding only slightly, as I pressed my fingers to my lips to prevent them from quivering. I glanced sideways to see Geertruyd eating from a paper cone she was holding while standing in the square and talking with neighbors, animated in their speech.

"Beatrice, it was difficult to remain in Mechelen. I wrote to Pope Leo while I was there. My family is in Firenze, and we know some of his de´ Medici relatives. I wrote to make him aware of what had happened with Father

Ardonne and Monsignor Bernardo. I told him of your father's murder and your near drowning," he continued.

The cacophony from the square was juxtaposed against our solemn, intimate conversation. "A short while ago," his voice lowered now so I could barely hear him over the crowd, "I received his reply. I have been excommunicated for interfering with Church matters and aiding a known enemy of the Church. Pope Leo wrote to my family and to the Haghenbeek family to inform them of the excommunication."

I put a shaking hand to my face and held the other out to the Duke. "What? No, no, this is my doing! Please allow me to make amends. I beg you! You must allow me to set this affair right." My hands shook as I held them out in front of my mouth.

"Beatrice, I have been told that the Church plans to seize and sell your father's tapisserie and house. I believe they plan to do it soon. They will probably send Ardonne and Bernardo to do it. I believe they plan to kill you."

The bells rang out and I covered my face, shaking with despair.

CHAPTER THIRTY ONE

Claire's Find

"This is about a rape," Mark repeated, nodding his head to agree with the Greek myth Artie had just read aloud.

Mark rose and began to pace, looking at Nora. His face looked haggard with purple and green splotches on his forehead and lips. His miserable glance seemed to be for Nora rather than himself.

He asked, "Nora, does this mean anything to you—a rape. This "within the nightingale sings." Within what? Is this something you may know from your studies?"

"No," she hesitated, but rose to pace with Mark. "No. Within what? Within the symbols? Like the myth, there's a story similar to Philomela in the symbols?" They both glanced at the tapestry, as if the answer would rise up from the threads and hover in the air.

I got up quickly from the couch saying, "Mark, what's inside a tapestry?" Leila looked up at the change in my voice.

Mark shrugged and looked up while thinking aloud, "Nothing. Knots, threads, and there's a linen or flax backing. There's really nothing inside. It just has a front and back."

"What are you thinking?" Artie asked. He knew my look.

I moved to the tapestry and turned it to see a pale, buff-colored flax backing. To Mark, I asked, "Can we rip this off?"

Both Nora and Mark extended their hands quickly and said "NO!" at the same time, as if to protect the tapestry from imminent attack.

"This is a priceless work of art. A perfectly preserved tapestry is phenomenally rare. In my profession I would be hanged for ruining something this unique," Mark said as best he could through swollen lips. He looked appalled at my suggestion while sounding possessive and protective.

"Well, maybe 'rip' was the wrong word," I admitted. Is there a way to take off the back to look inside without ruining it?"

Artie was beginning to see where I was going. Nora asked me to get my seldom-used sewing kit. I retrieved it from the closet.

"You do it," I said and handed a stitch-remover to Mark.

"Okay, but I'm not a conservator or restorer. I mean I know about conservation, but it's not my area of expertise," he said procrastinating. He looked around the room for help as if one of us would suddenly admit to being a closeted art conservator.

"Just do it," Nora said while waving her hand at the tapestry. "It's just a tapestry. Paolo is more important than this tapestry."

"Uh-huh. Like the *Mona Lisa* is just a painting. Like a Harley is just a motorcycle." Mark knelt next to the tapestry and touched the edge of the backing with delicate movements.

I saw his hands shaking a bit. He hovered over the backing, then he seemed to make up his mind.

He was tentative at first, removing just enough stitches to see inside the tapestry. He gradually opened the back to about a hands-breadth. He looked up at me with a puzzled expression.

"What? What?" I was down on my knees next to him while Nora and Artie crowded in next to me.

"Get me a flashlight," he said to no one in particular, and Nora was the first up. She opened my hall closet, found the light and smacked it a few times to wake up the batteries before she handed it to him.

He looked inside the tapestry and sat back on his heels, "Well, I'll be damned," he said.

Chapter Thirty-Two

The Duke's Dilemma

"They mean to kill you. I think we should leave tonight," the Duke replied as he pulled my hands away from my face. His face was gentle and filled with concern.

"We? Who is we? Leave for where?" I asked. I could not imagine what he was thinking. He must be mistaken.

"You and I. We must get the tapestry. My family has surely paid for it many times over," his voice was bitter. "We will ride out tonight. We will travel south to the Rhine, follow it to the Mediterranean and catch a ship to the Italian coast in order to reach Livorno. We will then travel along the Arno River to Firenze, where I believe we can hide. Though my family will not help me, I have friends who will. Perhaps I can sell the tapestry so we can make the trip."

"Hide? Catch a ship? Livorno? What are you saying? We cannot travel together, we are unmarried! I have no attendants. I am an unmarried maiden. It will take months to travel, and I have no fortune. Also, the tapisserie is mine. I intend to carry on with Father's weaving. You can't sell the tapestry." Did he not understand these things?

He looked at me without speaking. His face was lined with unhappiness.

"I cannot leave my home," I cried and reached out my hand to him in supplication.

His voice was quiet as he touched my skin. "Beatrice, you don't have a home."

CHAPTER THIRTY THREE

Claire Loses

Mark pulled the front and back of the tapestry apart slightly to show us that something was inside. We all peered in together, nearly knocking heads.

There was fabric within, covered in tiny writing. We couldn't see much more so Mark assigned each of us to pull threads at the corners in order to extend the openings.

He used the sewing tool to begin pulling threads at each corner to get us all started. We worked quietly. No one said a word. Leila's tail marked the time by smacking against the floor. Mark threatened to have us all executed if we tore the tapestry.

It took over an hour to remove the back without damaging the front of the work.

With the backing completely open and folded over on itself, we looked toward Mark to enlighten us. We could see a pale, white linen-looking fabric covered with black handwriting.

"It's writing," he said and then flushed for stupidly elucidating the obvious. "It's not English. Claire, what is this?" Mark looked to me for an answer.

I perused the miniscule handwriting. It was everywhere. It extended the length and width of the immense inner lining, resembling dark ants on a picnic blanket.

"It's Flemish, I think," I said, looking up at their faces, "I don't read Flemish well, but I recognize some words."

Nora turned to look at me. It was the first time she looked at me since entering the door this evening, and the first time her expression hadn't shown contempt. "Hey, doesn't your grandmother speak and read Flemish?"

I replied that she did, but that she probably would have difficulty with medieval text. I knew Grandma would surely give it a go. I asked about the time, not sure if she would be awake.

Artie looked at his watch and started to state the time, but a knock at the door gave us all pause and caused us to stare at the staircase. The door opened, footsteps creaked, and Simon's head appeared behind the stairwell.

Simon said nothing as he strode over to the tapestry. He looked down at it and then up at me. The room was very quiet. Even Leila sensed that this was no time to wag her tail. Simon looked tall and severe. The priceless tapestry looked limp with threads protruding on all sides.

He shook his head as he spoke while taking in the ravished tapestry on the floor, "I knew it." He said this while shaking his head over and over.

"I knew you would have it here. Claire, I'm taking the tapestry back to the evidence room," he lifted the tapestry from the floor as he spoke.

He stopped once he had the tapestry tucked under his

arm. He looked straight at me, ignoring the others in the room. "See me in my office tomorrow, Claire. You're fired."

He walked down the staircase with no resistance from any of us. When the door at the bottom of the stairs had closed, we all looked at one another. At first, no one spoke.

"I guess that was your boss," Mark said.

I took a deep breath and smiled. "Oh yes, that was Simon. Now he has the tapestry. We have nothing to show Grandma. We're finished. I'm finished. God, what a mess," I rubbed my eyes and temples.

"Not so fast," Artie grinned. He pulled a rumpled cloth from beneath the back of his shirt. "He has the tapestry, but I have the writing. I think we won this round."

"Ooohhh," Nora waved her arms and kissed Artie full on the lips.

"Wait, wait a minute," I said to both of them. "Artie, you do realize that Simon will fire you too when he finds out you took this? You don't need to do this."

Artie still had Nora attached like a barnacle. "I have my reasons. I want to see where this goes. I have a feeling I'm not here by accident."

Chapter Thirty-Four

The Duke Proposes
a Solution

When the Duke said I had no home, I swallowed hard and waved Geertruyd over to us. She must have known the Duke's business because she asked no questions; instead, she simply stuffed the apricot bun in her pocket.

The Duke directed her to bring extra clothes wrapped in plain cloth to St. John's Hospital. We would meet her there before leaving. Geertruyd pulled me close, and we embraced firmly. She must have known we would not meet again.

"How will you live, Beatrice? You have no family, no fortune, no work. What will you do?" she asked. She put her hands around my face, asking her earnest questions while knowing I had no answers.

"I believe the Duke is a good man, and he will not let

me starve. If I am able to find a home I will write to you," I promised. "But, you must never let the Church know where I have gone."

"Oh Beatrice, my reading and writing are not as fine as yours." Geertruyd's family had not taken an interest in educating their daughters.

"Have your father read my letters to you. I must go now." I kissed her hands, and we parted with reluctance. "Thank you for bringing me to the Duke. I believe you may have saved my life. Thank your family for their kindness to me. If I am ever able to repay them, I will send the florins needed to repay your father."

Geertruyd waved off my offer of repayment, walking away from us and the belfry toward my home. The Duke reminded her to be careful when retrieving the clothes and to leave if there was any sign of either Ardonne or Bernardo.

I turned to walk to St. John's Hospital. The Duke stopped me with an outstretched hand. "There is still one matter to resolve, Beatrice."

I was bewildered over everything: losing my Father, my sister, my home, my friend. What else could I resolve? I had resolved nothing. I was helpless.

"We cannot travel if we are unmarried," the Duke said. "Will you marry me, Beatrice?" He grasped my hands.

"Marry you?" I asked. I put my fingers to my lips to stop their trembling, but the tears came just the same.

"Has your fortune fallen so low that you ask for my hand, when you were promised to the cousin of Marie of Austria?" I felt I had brought this great gentleman down, just as I had brought about my own demise.

"My life is changing rapidly, as is yours. I do not pretend to understand why we have been forsaken by the Church we both revered at one time. But, you and I have been thrown together for some reason. I have loved you since the day Geertruyd stepped on the back of your skirt, making you unable to rise. I have loved every movement of your hands, your mouth, your eyes."

"When you move," he continued, "I take in every fold of your dress, and I smell sage about you. You have captivated me with every syllable."

"As a duke, there was no hope of marrying you. I had family obligations and a place in society. Hope for love was abandoned. My responsibility—my duty—was to my family," he said.

"But I am no longer a duke. My family has disowned me, Beatrice. I have no home and no family, just as you have none."

"We have a poet in Firenze, Dante Alighieri, who also had a love named Beatrice. Perhaps you have heard of him or read his writings. He wrote a sonnet so as to send Love to speak to Beatrice on his behalf. Love said of him, 'My Lady, his heart is fixed with so firm a faith, that all his thought is set on serving you—he was yours at first, and could not waver.'"

He continued with a broken voice, "Beatrice, my Beatrice, I was yours at first and could not waver."

We moved to one another there on the walk to the hospital, not caring if we were seen. Kisses flowed over eyelids, cheeks and mouth. My hands moved under his cape to feel his warm back. We held tight for a moment, but at length he pushed me away.

"Am I to believe you have accepted my proposal of marriage?" he asked, laughing. "We must go now. First we procure the tapestry, then we will meet Geertruyd for the clothing, and then we must leave Bruges."

I was both too happy to speak and too confused to understand how we would escape a place I had never left in my life. The farthest I had ever been was Ghent. How could I feel safe outside Bruges? How could I feel safe within Bruges?

We ran to the tapisserie first. It was late evening, and the tapisserie had been closed for hours. I had not been there since Father died. I had no idea if the tapestry was completed.

The apprentices, however, were loyal to Father's memory. The tapestry was rolled neatly with bands of fustian tied around it. It had been placed on a table near the door to the garden. It was safe, but I couldn't help but think about all the trouble that had arisen around this object lying quietly next to the garden door.

Only then did I feel I could tell the Duke what I had done. I explained how I had crafted Marie's story into the border and had later asked Jan to leave a tiny opening in the back for my diary to be fixed in between the front and back of the tapestry.

"Ah, my bright and beautiful Beatrice, no wonder the priests were after you. You are bound to tell Marie's story no matter what the price," he said laughing. We were both relieved to have come this far, rather than finding ourselves gazing down at flames while tied to posts.

The Duke picked up the tapestry easily, despite its weight. We moved through the garden quietly toward the street.

Two figures moved toward us—Ardonne and Bernardo!

"What do you want?" the Duke shouted to them and moved protectively in front of me.

"What you have in your hands. We are seizing what is now Church property. Or did you not know, Beatrice? All of what your father once owned belongs to the Church now to do with as we see fit."

Ardonne motioned to Bernardo to get the tapestry. He turned to me and added, "Your workers will feel the flames. They have all been executed inside the tapisserie for their part in this monstrous creation. The flames will take their putrid souls to hell, where they will soon meet your soul."

I heard a low moan emanating from my throat.

Just then Bernardo struck the Duke hard in the side of

the head with both hands swinging together like a mace.

The Duke struck the cobblestones face first. Ardonne picked up the tapestry and gave a signal to Bernardo, to which Bernardo walked to the garden gate and pulled a torch from the roadside. He broke the window of the tapisserie with the soup pot I had long ago left on the ground, and he then threw the torch into the tapisserie.

"No! No!" I screamed and lunged for the door. "No, Jan, Basil! Adolph! Dominicus! No, no, no!

The Duke arose from the cobblestones and put out his hand to stop me by pulling me to him. "You must let this go, Beatrice! They have won. You must stop. We have both lost everything. They are all gone. You must stop this!"

I sat down on the cobblestones weeping and screaming, tearing at my linen cap.

The Duke stumbled over to Ardonne and spoke inches away from his face, "You are a disgrace. No clergyman's robe can erase murder and arson from your soul. If there is a god, may he place you in the ninth circle of Hell to be frozen in Lake Cocytus as the Great Worm chews on your face for all eternity."

While they were turned I pushed the diary into the small opening Jan had left and prayed my words were safe.

CHAPTER THIRTY FIVE

Claire Receives a Message

Artie and Nora left somewhere around one in the morning. Mark looked miserable, his swollen lips protruding beneath tired eyes.

"Let's get you to bed," I said. "We can sleep late, and Art and Nora will meet us at Grandma's mid-morning. There's no reason to think about it anymore right now. Can you make it up to the bed?"

Mark sat down on the couch behind him. "No. I can't," he said, rubbing his forehead. "My head hurts, and I want to go to sleep."

I instructed him to use the couch and covered him with a warm blanket after taking off his shoes. His feet extended a bit over the couch, but he didn't seem to care. Leila sat next to him on the floor.

Since I was supposed to be on concussion watch, I figured I should sleep downstairs too. I went up to the loft, pulled the covers off the bed and brought them downstairs. I made up a bed on the floor next to Leila.

Suddenly all seemed right with the world. Later on grandma would read what was inside the tapestry, and it would vindicate Paolo. Nora would be back drinking iced tea in my kitchen. I would get my job back or maybe even be promoted—then again, probably not.

Mark moved slightly on the couch, rolling toward me. His arm lain over one side while absently petting Leila's ear, though his eyes were closed. I thanked the universe for bringing him in on this. He had taken a beating when the bookcase fell on him, but he hadn't given up. Mark had even given me advice on my bizarre family. He deserved a place on my couch and a portion of Leila's ear. I was exceedingly grateful to him.

In the morning I was up before Mark. He looked disheveled and discolored, but seemed to be sleeping soundly. I showered, ate and walked Leila. By the time I got back, Mark was already awake and showered. I gave him a yogurt and threw some berries in the bowl.

"You look better—do you feel better?" I asked, sincerely hoping there was no permanent damage. I felt personally responsible for his well-being.

"I feel lousy. You don't by any chance have an extra toothbrush, do you?" I was glad he asked because his smelly, bloody mouth was polluting the air in my tiny kitchen.

I watched him brush his teeth in the bathroom from my couch where one could see every corner of the apartment. "I want to thank you for doing this. It really is quite nice of you, especially after taking a beating from Mother Nature,"

I shouted over the toothbrush sounds.

He finished and came into the living room with a towel in his hands. "You're welcome, Detective. Other than the fat lip and headache, this is the most fun I've had in ages." He actually smiled, then grimaced and touched his stitches.

He went on, "You know, I can see why you care so much about Nora. She isn't going to give up on Paolo, and I really don't think she will give up on you. Your relationship with Nora and Art tells me you like to connect with solid, good people."

"I do," I agreed, but then again that seemed logical—didn't everyone?

"Would you...consider...connecting with me after this mess is finished?" he asked, towel in hand.

"I would," I said. "You'll just have to define 'connect' some time when I can give your definition my full attention. It sounds like something AT&T does."

We left for Grandma's. As it turned out, Mark lived nearby in South Laguna. The drive south on PCH was pleasant. The day was sunny with no clouds, as usual.

Mark and I talked easily. I prepared him for Grandma, whose accent was thick and delicious. She spoke a mélange of Flemish and English, or "Flenglish" as Mark called it.

"I think she'll like you," I predicted.

"Why is that?" he asked.

I noticed how nice he looked, now freshly scrubbed and more enthusiastic. He was a trooper.

"First, Grandma loves men. Second, Grandma loves witty, intelligent men," I informed him.

"Does she like fat lips?" he asked.

"She especially loves fat lips," I assured him. Knowing Grandma and Flemish remedies I had grown up with, she would probably meet him at the door with some kind of poultice made of chicken droppings.

Artie and Nora pulled up at almost the same time we did outside Grandma's house—a minuscule bungalow on the east side of PCH in South Laguna.

Her place had the best front garden on the block. Most of the time Grandma was there tending to roses and hydrangeas in a large, tattered straw hat. Though the garden was tiny, it was always on the Laguna Garden Tour. During the tour, I served iced tea under a rose arbor while Grandma explained how to keep hydrangeas blue.

She must have seen us from the front window. I had called her before we came to explain everything. She opened the door and, like any slightly hard-of-hearing person, shouted for all of us to come in.

I warned her on the phone that Dr. Davies had been hurt in the earthquake. Grandma had met Artie and Nora before at family barbeques. For family gatherings, I always invited everyone I knew as a buffer against my father.

Although Grandma and my mother looked alike, Grandma had all the *chutzpah*.

"Come en zee een, come en zee een," she waved to us. We crowded through the door, and Artie got to business immediately.

He pulled out the rough piece of white fabric with black ink on it. He explained briefly what we needed, which I had already told Grandma on the telephone.

Grandma pointed to iced tea and glasses on the coffee

table but talked only of the writing on the fabric. "Geff eet to me, Art," she said in her lilting accent. "Let me zee."

She told us she could read some of it, but warned there were words she didn't recognize. She began translating immediately as I wrote down, "I was sixteen years old when Marie died giving birth to Father Bernardo's child." It was a diary!

The story went on and on. The only sound in the room other than Grandma's voice was a soft ticking of the wall clock. We all became accustomed to Grandma's sweet accent. Somehow she took on the look and sound of a 16-year-old girl as she read aloud.

Grandma translated, "I knew I tasted my sister's death on my tongue," Artie got up and began to pace. His lips curled up, and he brushed over his mouth with his sleeve. He poured himself iced tea and downed the glass in one slug.

I watched him pace while I listened to Grandma at the same time. Artie looked more and more agitated as she translated. He sat, then stood, sat, then stood.

I sent him a 'what-is-it?' look, but he glanced away. He looked like he might be sick. As he walked sweat broke out on his face, and he swept his hands through his hair.

Grandma finished with the Duke's curse on Ardonne to languish in the ninth circle of Dante's Hell. She looked up at us, tired. "Dat's eet, no more," she said, with a wave of her wrinkled hand. She was once again my Grandmother, rather than a young girl.

We all looked at each other. There was a mix of relief and confusion—relief that Paolo had been vindicated but confusion about why the Church wanted the tapestry, as well as what ultimately happened to Beatrice and the Duke when they left Bruges.

We moved about the room mumbling about the diary content and what it meant. I made Grandma comfortable with a large glass of iced tea. She had been reading aloud for quite some time.

Suddenly a tall, well-dressed figure entered the room through the kitchen and moved toward us. Though the face was handsome, and the clothes expensive and foreign, I focused on the gun in his hand.

"Who the hell are you?" I demanded, feeling for my own gun.

"No, no," he said, with an accent. "No gun. I am Piero DiAlberto, an attorney. I come from the Vatican. Of course, I am here on a special mission of my own. The Holy Father doesn't condone this sort of thing." He said this as he waved his gun hand back and forth.

I moved in front of Grandma and noticed that Artie had positioned himself in front of Nora. Mark was at my side.

DiAlberto pointed the gun at Grandma. "What does it say about the money?"

"What money?" we asked in unison.

"There was no reference to money," I said. I looked around the room for another weapon and for a method of egress.

"The de´ Medici gold florins hidden in the Vatican, that's what money. Where are they? What does the tapestry say about where they are?" he asked.

He was tall, handsome, with pointy features. He appeared calm, almost numb.

"The tapestry doesn't mention anything about money. The diary mentions some nut job named Father Ardonne who believed that Pope Leo X had money hidden in the Vatican that belonged to Ardonne's family. That's all we know," I said.

"This is about money?" Artie asked in a guttural voice I had never heard him use before. "This is about money!" he shouted. His face was contorted with rage.

DiAlberto pointed at Artie with his gun and said, "Shut up!"

"Ardonne, we know about him at the Vatican. He was crazy. He was burned at the stake when Monsignor Bernardo reported Ardonne's plot to have Leo X killed and replaced. I want to know what he did with the money. For years we have kept this ugly tapestry Ardonne yammered on while he was tortured that he believed it contained a secret. All those florins he went on about losing. I want to know where they were hidden." He shouted the last sentence and waved the gun.

"All you people care about is money," Artie said, pointing a shaking finger at DiAlberto. "You've never cared about any one of your 'flock.'" Artie almost spit out the last word.

"Did you care about my brother? Did you?" Spittle was flying from Artie's mouth. His face was crimson. *What was he talking about?* He was making no sense.

"Who the hell is your brother?" asked DiAlberto, barely looking at Artie.

"Ryan," Artie said, his voice breaking with a stifled sob. "He was a victim too just like Marie, Beatrice, the Duke—all the rest! He was an altar boy. He was twelve. And he hung himself! Did you care about him?" Artie was screaming.

I had never seen Artie, nor any man I cared about, dissemble before. It was an awful sight. I wanted to go to him and hold him. Nora and Mark looked both concerned and appalled. It was as if we were watching a volcano erupt, but our feet were glued to the floor.

Artie shouted, "He was a boy who believed in the goodness of the Church, his priest and his fellow men! He was sexually abused by a *beloved* parish priest, but he told no one. When he hung himself in our garage, he left a note saying he could never tell anyone and couldn't bare the shame. Did you care about a hanged boy named Ryan?" Artie rubbed the tears from his cheeks with the cuff of his shirt sleeve.

My mouth hung open in disbelief. *Oh my god, poor Artie. Poor Ryan.*

DiAlberto ignored him and moved closer to Grandma, pointing the gun at her. "You are of no concern to me. I want the gold florins. They will be worth millions by now. Shut your face," he said over his shoulder to Artie, "and tell me where they are hidden."

Grandma put her hands to her neck and made gagging sounds. She'd had a stroke in the past. This man was causing her to have another. She shook violently, falling to the couch.

We all moved at once. Mark and I went for Grandma, as Nora lunged for DiAlberto and Artie kicked the gun out of his hand.

Grandma winked at me and smiled. I picked up DiAlberto's gun from the floor and pointed it in his direction. Nora had struck him sideways as Artie kicked him in the shins, and DiAlberto fell backward. Nora grabbed his hair on his way down and pulled with all her might. DiAlberto let out a wild scream as he fell back, half-sitting, with Nora still holding onto his scalp. He was stuck, and Nora wasn't letting go.

Artie took the opportunity to kick DiAlberto in his ribs several times as Mark sat atop the struggling, prostrate figure then Artie cuffed him to Grandma's coffee table. Artie was cursing in a steady stream inches from DiAlberto's face.

We all stood for a moment, looking at one another and breathing hard.

I moved to Artie to comfort him. "Art, I'm so sorry. I didn't know you had a brother. I'm so very sorry. How awful to lose a brother that way." I put my hand over his hand.

Artie suddenly sat down. He landed next to DiAlberto on the floor. He began to moan—an awful, frightening thing—while he rocked back and forth. The moaning escalated to full sobs, while we watched helplessly. His shoulders shook hard. He struck his fist against the floor.

"He was my brother," he cried and rocked. "My brother!"

Shuddering moans continued to escape him, and he put his hands over his face to block out the world.

After a few minutes he pulled his hands away from his face, but still rocked. He said more quietly, gently almost, while staring at the floor, "Those are his beads in my car. He was my hero. He wanted to be a veterinarian and a surfer. He played the drums. He liked chocolate ice cream with bananas, and he loved basketball. He liked life, until he met that damned priest."

Just like Marie—the forgotten ones. Oh the mess the Church had made of a sacred trust.

CHAPTER THIRTY SIX

Betrayal

Nora used my phone to call Simon. He brought over two black and whites. DiAlberto was taken away, still with an air of superiority about him.

Simon could see that Artie was in a state, so he said very little. As he left, Simon told Nora he would have Paolo released pending an investigation of the evidence and send him to meet her. She nodded.

We gave Artie space to mourn privately in Grandma's living room. I brought him a napkin for his nose and left a glass of water at his side. I held him around the shoulders until he seemed calmer. There were no words to say, so I didn't say any.

Grandma led the others outside to the garden. They would wait until Artie could pull himself together.

Thirty minutes later Artie came out of the house and walked to the garden. Grandma handed him an iced tea. Mark gave up his seat to Artie, and we indicated we were ready to listen. Artie's face was calmed, but swollen and red. His eyes were sadder than I had ever seen.

He told us tales of Ryan as a boy. He was three years older

than Artie, and Artie worshipped him. Ryan was a protector. Rather than torture his little brother, he was there to have his back. His death had devastated the family.

Artie found him in the garage. He had been calling Ryan for dinner. They were supposed to head to school together for a basketball game after dinner. His mother had sent Artie outside to see if Ryan was there or at a neighbor's house.

Artie called and called. He looked in the garage once and had seen only their green Chevy's bumper. Hours later he looked again and that time he saw Ryan's feet. Looking up, he saw the rest of Ryan hanging, his face purple with a urine stain on the front of his Penney's jeans.

The funeral had been held at the same church where Ryan had been abused. No one seemed to find this odd, Artie reported. No one seemed to acknowledge that Ryan was gone.

His mother began to drink heavily and his father retreated behind the newspaper. They didn't speak of Ryan. Artie had questions, but he wasn't allowed to speak Ryan's name. No one would talk to him about what had happened nor what would be done about it.

They continued to go to the same church, as if nothing had happened. Artie said he used to vomit before church on Sundays because he was so upset that one of the priests there, he didn't know which, might touch him during communion. The one who had been responsible, whoever he was, might greet his parents at the church door and deny by his very existence that Ryan had been wronged.

No wonder Artie spoke so little his family to me.

He continued, "When I heard DiAlberto dismiss what had happened to that girl in the tapestry and ask about money, I knew nothing had changed. The Roman Catholic Church will never change. The only reason they've acknowledged the sexual abuse is because the press made a stink."

"I was in therapy as a child and adult for years over this. *Years.* There's no place to go to hide from a suicide in your family. It's there every day when you wake up. I see his little body, and I remember trying to jump up to reach his shoes to give him support. Those are the memories I have every day."

"If I'd gone in the garage the first time—instead of stopping at the car bumper—if I'd known what to ask him, if I'd loaned him my baseball glove, would that have made a difference? Would he be alive? If I'd stopped him from being an altar boy, if, if, if. There's no end to the questions. And there are no answers."

"Finally, several years ago, I read somewhere that 'acts of judgment bind us to the past.' That made sense to me. After years and years of struggling with what happened to Ryan and my family, it made sense. I was bound to that awful memory of Ryan, hanging in the garage, and to the desire to kill that priest. It consumed me. It ate away at my present and future."

"Finally, I gave it up. I had to, or it would destroy me. Then there would be two victims. I might as well have hung myself next to Ryan, unless I could make it end. But, it all came back to me when DiAlberto walked in from the kitchen."

This was the most personal information I had ever heard

Artie speak in all the time I knew him. As partners we spoke in the car, but it was about our cases. I never knew Artie to speak of his family. I did remember him watching the beads swinging from the rear view mirror. That distant smile he gave wasn't for a woman, it was for his lost brother.

Grandma went to Artie, who seemed to be sitting taller now and taking some deep breaths. She kissed the top of his head. "Marie and Ryan will be in my prayers. I only pray to the good gods—the ones who watch over and protect their children," she said.

With her Flenglish soliloquy over, she waved goodbye to us. I knew she was headed in for a nap. She gave Artie another smile, kissed her fingertips and brushed them along Artie's cheek as she walked inside the house.

Artie looked tired, announcing it was time to head home. He would see me tomorrow. I wondered if he would be able to drive. He then stopped and said to me, "Jesus, Simon fired you."

"Oh yeah," I said. Oddly, I felt at ease about being fired. Or, I hadn't really been thinking about it. "I guess I'll see you when I clean out my desk. Come over after work and have a drink at my house, okay?"

Artie agreed. I didn't drink and he knew that, so a "drink" for him meant coffee with some liquor I had hidden away for parties. Artie liked fancy coffees with whipped cream on top, and I felt like he deserved an extra tall whipped cream. Mine would be a fancy coffee too, sans the liquor.

Nora headed out to meet Paolo. Before she left me, she thanked all three of us profusely. I could see she was sincere— exhausted—but sincere. I invited her to come over with Paolo when Artie came over after work tomorrow.

Since I drove, I asked Mark if he wanted to go home. He seemed relieved. He looked shell-shocked as well, as if Artie's pain had moved through all of us like lightning hitting a fence we were all gripping.

"I'll shower and see you later, possibly for dinner."

"Can you get food past those lips?" I asked.

"Damned straight," he said with a crooked smile filled with stitches.

I dropped him off, and then I went home to shower and nap. It had been an exhausting day, and Artie's revelation was so disturbing that I wanted to sleep—to think of nothing temporarily.

Leila napped with me, solid as a warm stone. Mark called later to invite me to his place for dinner.

He gave me directions, and I programmed them into my GPS: a gift from Simon when we had been an item. The evening was warm with breeze coming off the ocean, and the moon high in the still-blue sky.

Mark greeted me freshly showered and smelling like toothpaste. His lips were less swollen and turning a lovely shade of green. The stitches were sticking out at all angles. He hugged me, and I thought I heard a kissing sound pass my ear.

"Still afraid those lips will be caught in the crossfire?" I asked. He smiled, hands at the edges of his mouth for support during the smile, and then hugged me again. It was a long hug. A long hug for a long day in which we had both felt the intense pain Artie had unloaded. I felt a pat on my head. I was much more interested in a kiss.

"Come in." He led me through a smart, masculine space—a beige space. I felt immediately at home. The accents were black, but the substance was beige. *Just my style.*

We sat drinking in front of the fire, him with a red wine and me with a sparkling cranberry juice and lime. He said quietly, head down, "I felt so bad for your partner today. I don't have a brother. I wish I did. I see how much you love your sister, and it was obvious in the diary how much Beatrice loved Marie. I know you care a great deal for Art."

"Yes, I do," I answered. In my way I love Artie, and he loves me. We will always be there for each other, even if we were no longer partners. Ryan wasn't there any more to have his back, but I would be there to have Artie's back if he would let me.

"I don't think it's right that people like Marie and Ryan should just fade away. There have to be thousands of people like them," Mark said, swirling the red wine around the deep glass as he warmed the glass with his hands.

"Well, I don't think they all die," I conjectured. "Some of them must move past it. But then, maybe they don't. Maybe we just think they do until they hang themselves, like Ryan."

"I want to tell you something, Claire." He looked serious, and I felt uncomfortable. I like this man. It would be a shame if this had all been too much for him and we were over before we started.

"You know we talked about your family...," he started, looking at his shoes.

My heart sank. *Oh no. Not them.*

"I told you I had made myself a 'safe-house,' but I didn't tell you why." He looked up into my eyes while I recalled what he had said. It seemed a long ago, and at the time I had pretended not to pay much attention.

"Are you going to tell me now why you need a safe-house?" I asked.

"Yeah." He got up and paced. This was awful. Two tortured and sad men in one day. I had hardly ever seen a male reveal even the tiniest bit of personal information, and here were two men I cared about in one day spilling their guts in front of me.

"I, uh...I'm, uh..."

"Yes?" I prompted. He looked miserable.

"I'm very, very witch," I heard him say as he stopped pacing. *Witch? That couldn't be right.* His swollen lips made him difficult to understand.

"Did you say 'witch'?" I asked.

"Rich," he clarified, moving his swollen mouth carefully.

I was confused. "And you're telling me this why?" I sought understanding.

"I've met women who were all about money. They don't say they are—well, actually they do if you listen— but it's written all over everything they do, especially here in Southern California where wealth is such a badge. It's embarrassing. Sometimes they throw themselves at me. When I was younger, I actually married one of them. I was confused. I confused her lust for money with lust for me— love for me."

I watched him. This was a story he was pained to tell, though I wasn't sure why. Having money wasn't against the law. At least he wasn't a witch. I thought male witches had a different name, wicca or something like that. *Why was I thinking about witches?*

"For a long time I've found it difficult to trust the reactions of women around me. I love my work, it's my passion and my safe-house. Do you see what I mean?"

"Just exactly how rich are you?" I asked. I cringed at my tactlessness because I had been strictly raised and taught never, ever, to ask such a crude question.

"My father is the financier you hear about on television, Benjamin Davies." He nearly whispered it.

"Davies, Benjamin Davies...wait, the billionaire?"

"That one." He looked as if he admitted he wore women's clothing at night.

"Well, that is a surprise." A classic understatement, kind of like a classic sweater set, is nice every now and then.

"The way I see it, any woman who can look into my bloody mouth and call my lips kielbasas is probably not the kind who wants to wear designer clothes out to charity events each night to show off her jewelry."

"By the way," I admitted, "your mouth smelled disgusting when I looked in it."

We laughed throughout dinner. Some careful kissing followed. While frustrating, it foretold of better things to come.

CHAPTER THIRTY SEVEN

Claire and Simon

The next morning I walked to work for the last time up Avocado to Farralon. I thought about my job, Artie, and Simon on the way up the hill. I thought about Mark, Nora, Beatrice, Marie and Ryan.

I decided I was lucky. I had been given an opportunity to see the effect of resentment in a life—in several lives.

I wondered why some people are given opportunities to learn, to make a change and to turn their lives in a different direction while some people are not.

I know the Buddhists say that when the student is ready, the teacher appears—but, what makes the student ready? What if one is never ready? What if one is never a student? What if the teacher never appears?

I also thought about how it's not the mistakes we make that haunt us, but rather the judgment we face for those mistakes. It's the judgment that forces us to live in the past, just as Artie had said.

Artie and the story of Ryan, as well as Beatrice's story of Marie, show the destruction caused by resentment and shame. I saw it in my father, how it robbed him of a life and of fulfilling relationships. I will not let his legacy be one that would rob me of relationships. I will not be bound to that life.

By the time I reached the door of the Art Theft Detail, I had only a slight sensation of bittersweet loss—the loss of what, I wasn't sure.

I opened the door. Artie was at his desk. There had to be a protein bar near him somewhere. He looked normal again with his clothes crumpled and rumpled, so he was feeling better. I walked straight to Simon's office.

Simon looked handsome, but he seemed smaller than the last time I had seen him. I hadn't worked myself into a frenzy over meeting with him, nor allowed my habitual black and white thinking to prepare me for a battle.

I spoke first. "Good morning. I'm here to pick up my things."

Simon started to apologize about why he had to fire me. I stopped him. I almost felt sorry for him.

"I know," I said, "I understand." I felt both courageous and full of serenity at the same time.

He made no response. He stared.

"Simon, this case has given me a glimpse into a world I don't want to live in—one I've lived in too long. It's given me a picture of life built on bitterness and regret. I'm too passionate about life to throw it away on old, tired dramas. I plan to be very busy. I plan to, well, I don't know yet. There's a lot out there to do. I'll be very busy."

I got up, shook his hand, and moved to the door. "By the way, don't stick Arthur with Marjorie Wells. He really can't stand her. The hairspray makes him crazy."

I shut the door. I stopped at Artie's desk to tell him I would see him after work to make him the homemade coffee drink with extra whipped cream.

"Did he really fire you?" Artie asked, brows knit together in concern.

"Yep. He really did, and then I fired myself. See you later."

Paolo and Nora arrived at my place first. Nora was in a rare form, nearly manic with pleasure. She put snacks on the coffee table and gave Leila a new bone. Leila took it to a corner in case one of us wanted to take it away.

Paolo was gracious, but a bit quiet. There were rings of tiredness under his eyes. This must have taken quite a physical toll on him, yet he was dressed well.

He came over to me, took both hands and kissed my fingertips while in a slight bow. I think he was trying to find words of thanks, but English wasn't coming into his head. I nodded while saying he was welcome and not to mention it, even though he hadn't gotten a word out.

Nora embraced us in a group hug. She looked straight at me and said, "I'm so grateful to you. I'm sorry I was awful. You, Artie and Mark were amazing. Paolo and I want to have a party for the five of us once we've recovered. Your friendship is everything to me. I'm so glad things can get back to normal."

And things would get back to normal. I would see to it. No resentment. It was important to let Nora know that I wouldn't hold this inside.

Artie arrived with a goat cheese and onion pizza. The

smell was fabulous, causing Leila to hover after abandoning Nora's bone. Artie looked better—he was a welcome sight in clumpy jeans and an unpressed shirt. He looked calm, though maybe a bit worn around the eyes.

Mark was last to arrive. He gave me an air kiss close to my ear. Nora saw it, and Artie started to snicker. I would have to make a lunch date with Nora to catch her up on all the details, not that there were many, though Artie had a look saying he already knew all he needed to know.

Mark set down a large vase of sunflowers bursting with deep, yellow blossoms and accentuated by purple phlox. When he handed me a package of kielbasa to grill, I think my drink came out of my nose.

We still felt the need to decompress, so we reviewed the events of the last few days. We went over them from every angle.

I realized the diary hadn't mentioned what happened to Beatrice and the Duke. I asked Paolo if he knew any details.

"I know only that the Duke lived in Florence, but separately from the rest of the family. He married Beatrice, though before yesterday I didn't know anything about her specifically other than her name. They had three children, and they ran a successful wool trade out of Florence. I know nothing else about them or their children," Paolo said.

I smiled inwardly. So Beatrice and the Duke married and had children. I also wondered if Beatrice had ever found peace of mind, or if she instead forever yearned for retribution.

Artie put on the news. There was Simon being interviewed. Nora groaned, rolling her eyes. Paolo gave her a hug.

We all watched as Simon bent toward the microphone, a bit too close to the blonde reporter.

"Today Detective Arthur Grey of the Newport Beach Art Theft Detail closed a case involving a tapestry reportedly stolen from the Vatican. After careful review of the provenance of the tapestry, Detective Grey was able to substantiate Mr. Paolo Campezzi's claim that the tapestry belonged to his family, rather than to the Vatican. Mr. Campezzi has been released from custody, and we have arrested Piero DiAlberto—a Vatican attorney—for charges related to the case," he said.

The announcer went on, repeating what Simon had said and filling in details about Paolo's family in Florence. He also added that Dr. Mark Davies, who had helped Detective Grey with the investigation, was the son of billionaire financier, Benjamin Davies. My part in the case was not mentioned.

Upon the announcement of Mark's family fortune, everyone turned to him, mouths open. "Yeah, well, who cares?" Mark said, raising both hands, palms up at shoulder height.

Artie shook his head. He told me that Simon would never admit to my participation in the successful culmination of the case because he would open himself up to the charge that I had stolen the evidence.

Mark drifted over to ask Artie to talk with him. Mark had discussed his plans with me the night before, so I knew what he was saying. Mark's family had a charitable foundation run by a non-family member. He wanted Artie to petition the foundation for funds in order to fund a support group

235

for people who had been abused by clergy.

I saw Artie turn his head suddenly to Mark and hold out his hand to shake while grabbing Mark's shoulder with the other hand. Artie shook his hand repeatedly and pounded Mark's shoulder. His lips were pressed together in a smile that could at any time dissolve into sobs.

Nora watched them and asked me what was up. I informed her. Her eyes filled with tears. She nodded her head up and down for several minutes, looking over at Artie. Mark and Artie still had their heads together, arms gesticulating as if their plans were already taking form.

"What are you going to do now, Claire?" Nora asked with concern in her voice for my job and future.

"I'm not sure, but I'm interested in consulting on museum security," I replied. "I haven't figured out the details yet, but I know people in the business, and so do Artie and Mark. I think it's all good."

"Let me put on some music for you while I grill the kielbasas," I announced to everyone. I went to the CD player to put on a new favorite song. I began to sway my hips to the rhythm as I moved toward the kitchen. Nora and I danced together.

Artie turned immediately from his conversation with Mark, "What is that caterwauling, DeMaer?"

I turned in reply, "It's 'The Snake' by the Mediaeval Baebes." It was a beautiful composition with a Medieval style sung by twelve women who comprised the group.

The piece had what sounded like a Moroccan drum beat, though I guessed it to be medieval Spanish. It conjured up gaily dressed women tossing flower petals while dancing.

For all I know it could have been about an ax murder, but it sounded joyful.

"Why are you playing something like that? The Mediaeval Baebes...," Artie looked perplexed at my choice.

"It's for Marie," I said.

"Oh, well, that's okay," Artie turned back to Mark.

I spotted a wrapped gift for me on the table. It had the shape of a book and was wrapped beautifully in gold ribbon and wrapping paper. I pulled off the paper to reveal a book of late Medieval poetry by Vitorria Colonna. I didn't know this author. I caught Mark's eye and held the book up. He smiled and nodded.

I opened it to a poem entitled "Why Endlessly Appeal to Death's Cold Ear?" I read through it and took special notice of the final stanza:

It only remains to see
if I am yet sane enough to turn crazed
hopeless desire into better deeds.

It's a process, I thought. It's a process.

THE END

Note from the Author

I've thoroughly enjoyed my experience in writing this book. I hope that it brings you as much joy as it did me. This book was a labor of love for five years. I visited Stirling Castle in Stirling, Scotland, as well as the Cluny Museum in Paris, the Victoria and Albert Museum in London, and the Metropolitan Museum of Art in New York in order to observe the marvel of tapestry. I endeavored to bring to you, the reader, the excitement I felt at seeing various remarkable tapestries in those picturesque places.

Look for the next book in my historical mystery series, visit me at pastaes.com.

Characters and Terminology

16TH CENTURY:

Flemish methods of personal address:

Meniere - Mr.

Mejuffrouw - Miss

Mevrouw - Mrs.

1520 measurement term: "ell" = approximately 27 inches (68.5 centimeters)

FICTIONAL CHARACTERS:

Beatrice van Hecke - daughter of Cornelius, younger sister to Marie

Cornelius van Hecke - Father of Beatrice, master weaver (tapissier)

Marie van Hecke - daughter of Cornelius, older sister to Beatrice

Geertruyd - friend of Beatrice

Father Bernardo - priest

Father Philippe Ardonne - priest

Duke Giulio Campezzi - Duke of Florence (Firenze)

Cecilia Haghenbeek - betrothed to Duke Campezzi

Mevrouw (Mrs.) DeGroot, former neighbor of van Hecke family, living at Begijnhof de Wijngaard (home of Beguin nuns, founded 1245 by Countess of Flanders)

Non~Fiction characters:

Pope Leo X – second son of Lorenzo de' Medici (papacy 1513-1521)

Pieter de Pannemaker - master weaver

Pieter van Aelst- master weaver

Rafael - cartoon(picture beneath tapestry) artist

Charles V - Holy Roman Emperor 1519-1556

Margaret of Austria - daughter of first Holy Roman Emperor, patron of the arts, guardian to nephew Charles V

21ST Century:

Fictional characters:

Claire DeMaer - detective, partner to Arthur Grey

Arthur Grey - detective, partner to Claire

Nora Fitzsimmons - interior designer, friend to Claire

Paolo Campezzi - distant relative of Duke Giulio Campezzi

Mark Davies, Ph.D. - museum curator, textile expert

Grandma - Claire's maternal grandmother

Valerie and Jim DeMaer, Annette DeMaer - parents and sister of Claire

Maizie - daughter of Claire's landlord

Simon Bayles - Art Theft Detail Captain

Susan Price - assistant to Dr. Davies

Roy - assistant to Dr. Davies

Piero DiAlberto - Vatican attorney

Resources

Alighieri, Dante. *La Vita Nuova*. Trans. A.S. Kline http://www. poetryintranslation.com/PITBR/Italian/TheNewLife. htm, 200-2002

Blaeu, Joan. *Atlas Maior of 1665*. Los Angeles: Taschen, 2005. Print.

Cesati, Franco. *The Medici—Story of a European Dynasty*. Firenze: Mandragora, 1999. Print.

Delmarcel, Guy. *Flemish Tapestry*. New York: Harry N Abrams, Publishers, 2000. Print.

Een Notabel Boecxken Van Cokeryen. *A Notable Little Cookery Book*. Thomas VanderNoot, printer. Circa 1514. Web.

Ferguson, George. *Signs & Symbols in Christian Art*. New York: Oxford University Press, 1954. Print.

Impelluso, Lucia. *Nature and Its Symbols*. Trans. Stephen Sartarelli. Los Angeles: J. Paul Getty Museum, 2004. Print.

Longfellow, Henry Wadsworth. "Carillon, Poem of the Belfry in Bruges." 1845. Print.

Martinelli, Giuseppe. *The World of Renaissance Florence*. Trans.

Walter Darwell. Florence: Giunti Gruppo Editoriale, 1999. Print.

Mediaeval Baebes. "The Snake." *The Rose.* Nettwerk, EMI Classics, 2002. CD.

Rawson, Hugh. *Wicked Words: A Treasury of Curses, Insults, Put-Downs, and Other Formerly Unprintable Terms from Anglo-Saxon Times to the Present.* New York: Crown Publishers, 1989. Print.

Additional Resources
for the Reader

I f readers would like to see real tapestries made as they were centuries ago, please feel free to visit Stirling Castle in Stirling, Scotland. At the end of a cobbled walk (past a lovely cafe in the castle) down a windy path, you will arrive at a warm and cozy glass structure, near the Nether Bailey, filled with talented weavers. The magnificence of their work is something one must see to appreciate.

In the 17th century, weaving moved from Belgium to France for a variety of reasons. To see French tapestry weaving in action visit Gobelins in Paris, and be sure to take a friend who speaks French.

To see both an original cartoon by Rafael and the final woven tapestry commissioned by Leo X, visit the Victoria and Albert Museum, London, or www.vam.ac.uk.

The Los Angeles Police Department's art theft detail is the only full-time detail of its kind in the United States. The Newport Beach detail is purely fictional. Visit www. lapdonline.org/art_theft_detail to read about the work of the detail's detectives and the antics of "stupid" art criminals.

For information about surviving sexual abuse by priests—there is help out there. Please check with your local CHAPTER of SNAP (Survivors Network of Those Abused by Priests) at www.snapnetwork.org to locate support systems, and please find a therapist in your area through your local mental health department.

For remarkably beautiful images of Bruges the reader may refer to http://members.virtualtourist.com/m/p/m/3462cc/ or better yet, make a visit to this stunning city.

1893616R00147

Made in the USA
San Bernardino, CA
16 February 2013